Parker's Passion

A Tryst Island Erotic Romance

SABRINA YORK

DEDICATION

This book is dedicated to Hollie Rieth and Lynnie Stringer. When you read the book, you'll know why, if you don't already.

ACKNOWLEDGMENTS

First of all, thanks to my amazing beta readers Tina Reiter, Carmen Cook, Angela Lane, Fedora, Nita Banks and Pansy. And to my amazing street team—Charmaine Arredondo, Crystal Benedict, Crystal Biby, Kris Bloom, Kim Brown, Sandy Butler, Jodi Ciorciari Marinich, Celeste Deveney, Tracey A. Diczban, Shelly Estes, Stephanie Felix, Joany Kane, C. Morgan Kennedy, Angie Lane, Tina LaRue, Rose Lipscomb, Chris Lewis, Kathleen Mixon, Laurie Peterson, Tina Reiter, Hollie Rieth, Regina Ross, Dee Thomas, Sheri Vidal and Michelle Wilson, as well as the shy ones, Christy, Elf, Fedora, Gaele, Hotcha, Laurie, Pansy Petal and Rae—for their support of my books and writing.

My deepest appreciation to Wicked Smart Designs for a rocking cover—always gorgeous—and to Monica Britt for helping me whip this novella into shape.

My heartfelt appreciation to my fellow writers for their support. Especially Kayelle Allen, Avery Aster, Sara Brookes, Emily Cale, Cassandra Carr, Cerise DeLand, Delilah Devlin, Adrienne deWolfe, Laurann Dohner, Tina Donahue, Lisa Fox, Gabrielle Holly, Desiree Holt, Jennifer Kacey, Ditter Kellen, Shelbie Knight, Adriana Kraft, Kathy Kulig, Cait Miller, Danita Minnis, Eloreen Moon, Nicole Morgan, Ana Morgan, Beverly Ovalle, Rebecca Royce, Chandra Ryan, Erin Simone and Zenobia Renquist.

To all my friends in the Greater Seattle Romance Writers of America, Passionate Ink and Rose City Romance Writers groups, thank you for all your support and encouragement.

CHAPTER ONE

It was a shock to the system, seeing him again, in the flesh, after all these years.

Kaitlin Stringer sat, stock-still in the uncomfortable chair in the cafeteria of the heaving ferry and stared. Just stared. Though she was surrounded by her friends, bathed in their protective presence, she felt vulnerable, raw.

A memory flooded her mind. A memory she never wanted to have again.

A young, stupid girl, a little too tipsy at a party. Lured into a back room. Surrounded by men. Cornered. Trapped.

And hands. Touching her. Everywhere.

She shuddered and forced the images from her mind, the panic from her soul. She drew in a deep breath and visualized a white light surrounding her, shielding her, insulating her. Peace descended.

She was safe.

She wasn't that stupid girl anymore.

"Are you okay?" Large brown eyes concerned, Jamie leaned over and gently touched her hand. Kaitlin winced as sensation invaded her, scored her. Visions flickered through her mind like a disjointed movie. *A wine spill at a recent gallery opening—on a painting. A flat tire. The fight with her boyfriend.*

Kaitlin jerked away, though she tried to pretend she did not, and slipped her hand under the table to rub the spot Jamie had touched. It burned. "Yes, I'm fine," she said "Just a little sea sick, I think."

A lie, but a forgivable one.

1

It wasn't often she was knocked askew like this. Not often she let her guard down. Not often the energies swirling around her found entrance and barged in.

She knew what it was. Seeing *him* again. It staggered her.

Deliberately, she thrust him from her mind and focused on her friends, Jamie and Tara who sat by her side, chatting about inane things and eating pastries, as though they hadn't a care in the world. Then again, they didn't.

Jamie riffled her short brown hair with a chuckle. "I know what you mean. Ferry rides get me every time."

"It probably wouldn't be so choppy if it were a larger boat," Kaitlin said. The ferry to Tryst Island was the smallest in the fleet.

Tara glanced up from the papers she was reviewing "I don't know what you two are talking about," she gusted. "I love it. It's like a mini cruise."

Kaitlin bit back a smile. Everything was an adventure to Tara. And why not? She was a bright, fearless girl with a lovely, vibrant aura. There were no nasty memories lurking in her eyes. Nothing terrible had ever happened to her.

"I can't wait to get there," Kaitlin said. "I really needed this." Her volunteer work at the shelter—while she reveled in it, loved really making a difference for the homeless women who came in—had depleted her reserves. It had been a tough week. She needed to recharge. At that thought, she rummaged in her bag until she found her chocolate, broke off a chunk and popped the rich square into her mouth. Almost immediately, she felt her tension ease.

"I hear ya, *sistah*." Tara tossed back her long dark ponytail. Something flickered over her expression, a minor tightening, but Kaitlin noticed it.

"Is everything all right?" she asked, focusing in. Tara's colors went from pink to dark ruby with green swirls, and then faded back to pink again.

"Just peachy."

Kaitlin could *taste* the lie, but she didn't pry. She took Tara at face value. She'd found, in her experience, it was the best way to play it. If Tara wanted to share what was bothering her, she would. And people so rarely *truly* wanted to share. She was used to their tiny prevarications. Good gravy, she was guilty enough of that herself.

She shot a glance at Jamie and something in her expression

snagged Kaitlin's attention. "Why are you smiling like that?" she asked.

Jamie batted her eyelashes. Whenever Jamie batted her eyelashes, she knew something. Something good.

Kaitlin leaned in, anxious for a diversion. And Jamie was always diverting. "Spill."

"Are you saying *you* don't know?" Jamie's eyes sparkled.

"I don't know everything."

"Don't you?" Tara quipped. She riffled around in the Stud Muffin bag and pulled out a pastry, then turned her attention to Jamie. "So what is it?"

Jamie tucked a brown curl behind her ear. Her aura glowed. "It's Cam and Kristi."

"Yes?"

"They're *together* now."

"Together?" Tara bit into the pastry and it crumbled. "What do you mean? Like together, together?"

"Yup."

Kaitlin blinked. "Really?" She'd sensed something simmering between her friends, but Kristi had insisted nothing would ever happen. Like ever. Kaitlin was glad she'd been wrong. The two were perfect for each other.

"Apparently, a couple weeks ago, they both went to the island and poof! Magic happened."

"That's awesome," Tara said.

"They're already there. Went over on Thursday. To have some *couple time* before the whole crew gets there." Jamie waggled her brows. "I think we should tease them mercilessly."

"Definitely." Tara chuckled.

"Who else is going to be there this weekend?" Kaitlin asked. She hadn't checked the online calendar before coming.

"Bella, Holt and…Drew." Jamie took a sip of her coffee to hide a grin. Her sly glance at Kaitlin, however, could not be hidden.

A flush crawled up Kaitlin's cheeks. Drew Boone, a hunky fireman with a handsome face and charming grin, was one of her best friends. He was adorable and so easy to be around—most of the time. And he was totally in love with her.

She knew it.

Didn't need to be psychic to know it.

Everyone knew it.

He followed her like a puppy dog. And flirted ruthlessly.

He flirted with everyone, but Kaitlin knew he was serious when he flirted with her. She saw it, the change in the colors swirling around him. But she'd never encouraged him.

It wouldn't be fair.

Not with her…issues.

Drew deserved a woman as open and generous as he was, someone who could give as good as she got. Kaitlin was not that woman. Aside from that, Drew deserved a woman who could love him with wholehearted passion.

And while she did love him, it wasn't in that way. And it never would be.

Kaitlin had accepted the fact that she would probably never have a physical relationship with a man; she would never be able to let someone that close. A simple touch was painful enough.

She'd tried once, with a nice, gentle guy named Kenneth she'd met at work. They'd dated for a while and when he kissed her, she'd let him. It had not been pleasant. She'd closed her eyes and tried to endure his touch. But in the end, before anything had really happened, she'd stopped him. It was just too much to bear. She couldn't imagine tangling intimately, emotionally, spiritually with someone.

Which was fine. Everyone had their own path. Hers, she would walk alone.

She had a gift—she could truly help others. But that gift came at a cost.

The fourth member of their party, Kaitlin's best friend Emily, burst into the cafeteria in a halo of white light and slid into the open seat at their table, her blonde curls bouncing. Emily was always a bundle of energy, but it was a soft and inquisitive energy, so she was a delight to be around. She gusted a sigh. "Douche alert."

"Where?" Jamie took a big bite of her pastry. The delicate crust flaked all over her t-shirt. She brushed the crumbs onto the table.

Emily blotted the ones that landed on her plate. "Out on the deck. He's wearing an ascot."

Kaitlin frowned. She'd run into that guy earlier. He'd cornered her in the hall. The vibes coming off him—the nasty snarl of malevolence—had seriously creeped her out. Nearly panicked her.

She'd had to spill her coffee on him to escape.

She'd learned that. Always carry a weapon.

Not a weapon to wound; hurting people wasn't in her makeup. But some people needed to be kept at a distance.

Even now, something prickled up her neck. She scoped out the cafeteria, then stilled as the guy with the ascot entered. And yeah. The colors around him were dark and sinister. She shivered.

He crossed the deck, his predatory eyes scanning everyone with a scowl. His malice was so prevalent, it trailed behind him in a murky cloud.

When he threw himself into a seat next to *him*—the guy she'd seen earlier, the one she'd recognized—her belly dipped. They *knew* each other. She wasn't sure why, but that fact disappointed her.

She studied the knot of men on the other side of the ferry. Handsome and entitled, with a cocky air about them.

She knew the type.

"Goddamn frat boys." She didn't mean to say it with such vitriol. But seeing him again had brought all the old bitterness back.

Her tone caught Emily's attention. "Do you know them?"

"Yeah." Oh, yeah. Her pulse hitched. She fiddled with her napkin. "Maybe. The good looking one went to U-Dub."

Jamie's brow wrinkled. "Which one is the good looking one?"

Right. With the exception of Ascot Man, they were all far too attractive for their own good. "The one with the spiky hair." With the sharp square chin, brown eyes that slanted a bit at the corners and an aura with a purple hue.

"Which one with the spiky hair?"

With a sigh Kaitlin realized both the men sitting in the corner with the creepy guy had identical haircuts. Typical herd mentality. "The one with the dark hair. In office casual. I think his name is…Parker." She knew damn well his name was Parker. She would never forget it. "I met him at a frat party once—" She trailed off and everyone waited for her to finish, but she didn't. She couldn't. She stared at her threaded fingers, willing herself not to look at Emily. Willing herself to reel in her thoughts.

She knew thoughts and memories weren't contagious, but energy was energy and could be transmitted to others. The last thing she wanted to do was remind Emily of *that* night. They'd gone together to the party, excited to have been invited. Not knowing what those boys had planned. That night had shifted the trajectory of both their lives.

It was annoying, those times when life surprised her. But for all that she could see and know things about other people, she was curiously blind when it came to herself. And that night…that night there had been no warning. None at all.

Jamie blew out a sigh as a raucous cheer went up from that corner of the cafeteria. "I hope it's not a rowdy weekend."

Kaitlin stilled as a premonition slithered through her. She skated a glance around the table at her friends. It swelled. Grew.

And she knew. She just knew.

Something was going to happen this weekend. To each one of them.

Something profound.

Parker Rieth slopped a dollop of whiskey into his coffee. Even as he did, he knew he shouldn't. He wasn't much of a drinker, but this had been a brutal week. Hell, a brutal month. The tension over the looming partnership had acid spitting in his gut. He deserved the promotion. Needed it. Had worked like hell for it. But there was always the chance that Barstow and Rank would choose Nate instead.

He took a sip of his laced coffee in an attempt to still his disquiet.

God, he needed a break. A blow out. A balls to the wall party weekend with no depositions, no briefs, no courtroom squabbles. No games.

He loved his job. Really, he did. Loved the challenges. Really loved winning.

But sometimes it got to him.

So when his buddy Ash had invited him to come over to his place on Trystacumseh Island for the weekend with buddies from college, of course he'd agreed.

He hadn't known Richie was coming when he'd agreed.

Richie was a peckerwood.

They'd roomed together in college for one quarter. It had been all Parker could take.

He and his friend Devlin snorted as Richie let out an ear-splitting whoop. The fucker was already drunk. "This weekend is gonna *rock!*" he bellowed. Then he leaned in and whispered, far too loudly. "I've already scoped out the chicks. Some hotties over there." He jammed his thumb at the table of women on the far side of the room.

Parker nodded, but didn't look. Didn't need to. He'd already seen them. Seen *her*.

Beautiful. Ethereal. Delicate.

She had an elfin face and soft red hair that curled in lush masses over her shoulders. Her figure made his mouth water. When she got up to refill her coffee cup, he found his gaze unaccountably snared by the curves of her ass in her jeans.

She was a woman who could entice a man to madness and therefore—in theory—should be avoided like the plague.

All he did, all day long, was help rich guys untangle their mistakes and wonder how someone so smart could be so stupid.

But one glance at *that* woman and he could see it. How a guy could go crazy. Sink himself into lust and forget everything else. Everything that mattered.

Like a condom. Or a pre-nup.

Well, that would never happen to him. He would never be so blinded by the emotion women called love that he would forget the essentials.

He was careful.

Always careful.

Dispassionate to a fault, that was Parker Rieth. That was what made him one of the top divorce attorneys in the state. Find a jugular and go for it, that was his motto.

A familiar tension tightened his shoulders and a twang of pain coiled at the base of his neck. He rubbed his left eye, hoping to stave off the migraine, and took another snort of his drink. Alcohol helped sometimes. But sometimes it made things worse.

She laughed. And—even though she was on the other side of the cafeteria, and even though he was deliberately facing the other direction, and even though he had no business even knowing it was her laugh—he grimaced as lust, and hunger for something else entirely, curled through him.

Jesus, he needed to get laid.

It had been a long time. Far too long, if just the sound of her laugh could make his cock surge.

He glanced over his shoulder as the thrum of the engine changed, marking their approach to the island. She stood and hefted her bag over her shoulder, flipping her hair out of the way. The strap of her purse rested between her breasts, outlining them in her filmy blouse. His fingers curled into fists.

She was just the kind of woman he should never be with.

Exactly the kind of woman he should avoid.

Damn.

CHAPTER TWO

Darby's Bar and Grill was hopping. It always was on Friday nights, but tonight it was busier than usual. Kaitlin stepped into the darkened cave. It pulsed with the music from the jukebox, hummed with the clamor of the crowd. The cacophony slammed into her like a wave.

She hated crowds.

If she was with a small group of friends, she could interpret all the conflicting and colliding energies, but in a place like this it could be overwhelming. Jamie, who understood, rubbed her back, urging her forward.

They'd gone straight to the house from the ferry dock to find a note taped to the sign-in board. *"Gone Drinkin'."* So they'd staked their claims on bedrooms and headed over to Darby's. There was no question where everyone had gone. There was only one bar on the island.

Kaitlin saw her friends seated at a large table on the restaurant side of the establishment—Kristi and her sister Bella, along with Cam and Holt. She waved. As they made their way through the crowd, Kaitlin's steps stalled when she saw Holt's arm around Bella's shoulders. She glanced at Jamie. "I thought you said it was Cam and Kristi," she murmured.

Jamie shrugged.

Apparently a lot had happened recently. "Sheesh," she said in an undertone. "Miss a couple weekends…" And Jamie laughed.

They all settled in and exchanged pleasantries but nobody

mentioned the two *bona fide* couples that had suddenly erupted in a group of longtime friends. The shift in energy was obvious to Kaitlin. With Cam and Kristi it was a calm, comfortable swirl. But the patterns around Bella and Holt bubbled with tension.

Sexual tension.

Kaitlin nibbled her lip and pretended to study the menu—though she could have recited it blindfolded. Sometimes it was awkward, knowing things. Seeing things. Things that were none of her business. Like the fact that Holt was hard. And that Bella was thinking about luring him into the bathroom for a blowjob—

Yeah, sometimes she wished her gift had an off switch.

The heat those two were giving off made her restless.

It was a relief when the waitress, Charmaine, brought their water. Kaitlin drank hers down immediately.

A ruckus erupted on the other side of the restaurant as a drunk patron tipped his chair too far back and fell to the ground. Raucous laughter rang out. Kaitlin froze as she recognized the creep from the ferry. He stood and brushed himself off and shot a dark look around the room. Their gazes clashed. Something that felt like panic writhed in her soul.

Stay away from him! Her instincts shouted. *Danger. Danger.*

And then some force drew her attention away, to the left, and she saw *him*. Parker. She hadn't expected to see him again so soon. Sure, it was a small island, and this was the only restaurant. But for some reason, she just hadn't expected it. Her heart thundered. Her vision blurred. Another premonition whipped through her, but too powerful and too quick to grasp. It left her breathless. "Jesus," she whispered.

Tara curled her nose. "Who are those guys?" she asked.

Holt glanced over his shoulder. "Ash Bristol."

"He has a place next to ours," Cam added.

Kristi nibbled her lip. "They look familiar."

Cam took a sip of his beer. "They went to the U-Dub. Ash is a friend of Lane's. I think the guy with the short hair is Parker…"

"Rieth." Kaitlin said when Cam struggled for the name.

"I don't know the guy in the ascot," Cam added. Everyone snorted. Because he was wearing an ascot. And who wore an ascot? "But the other guy is Devlin Fox."

Next to her, Tara stiffened. The halo around her fizzled and snapped. "That's *Devlin Fox?*" she spat.

All heads swung in her direction.

Kaitlin focused in on Tara's colors. Warning bells clanged.

"You know him?" Bella asked.

Tara glared around the table. "He writes a Foodie Blog. He gave Stud Muffin a bad review."

A chorus of dissention rose. "Why did he do that?"

"Because I don't have gluten free." She crossed her arms over her chest and glared at the table across the room. Her annoyance crackled. And then she muttered under her breath, "Baby."

Because she was watching, Kaitlin saw it. A dark slither of bitterness curled from Tara's heart chakra and wrapped around her. It bloomed and spiraled out, toward Devlin. "What are you thinking?" she asked in a whisper.

Tara froze and shot her a frown. Then she forced a smile. "Nothing." She made it a point to bat her lashes.

A lie. A big fat lie. But Kaitlin didn't say anything. There was no point in calling her out. She needed to keep her eye on Tara this weekend though. The premonition she'd had earlier still clung to her. Her attention skipped from Tara to Jamie and Emily.

Good gravy, it was annoying, only getting part of the picture. What was the point of a warning if the stupid universe didn't tell you what the warning was about?

Her gaze was drawn back to the men's table. It stalled on Parker and something rippled up her spine. Discomfort rose, clogging her throat, nearly choking her with dread. *Fire. Flames. Burning flesh.*

Oh yes. She was going to have to be on her guard this weekend, if she was going to keep her friends from disaster—whatever that disaster was.

Kaitlin felt Tara's energy seethe as she stared at Devlin, muttering under her breath.

It would help if they would cooperate.

After the ferry docked Parker and Richie hopped in Devlin's car, drove over to Ash's place and dumped their stuff. Parker was glad it wasn't far because they'd all been drinking. So he suggested they walk to the bar where their friend was waiting for them.

Ash greeted them with a wave and a grin.

Damn, it was good to see him. Despite the vast differences in their upbringings, Ash Bristol was his best friend, practically a brother. When Parker had been all alone in the world, Ash's family had embraced him, given him roots. Given him hope. They'd shown him the world wasn't a huge, hostile place.

He had no idea where he'd be, if not for the Bristols.

Dead in a gutter, probably. With a needle in his arm.

Parker slid into his seat. When he nearly missed it and almost landed on the floor, he decided it was time to back off on the whiskey and get some food in his belly. Yeah. They'd probably all started drinking too early. Richie was listing to the side.

After they gave their orders to the spunky waitress, he turned to Ash. "So, how's everything going?"

Ash shrugged and took a sip of his beer. "Going good. How about you? Heard anything about the promotion?" They hadn't seen each other in a while—life got so busy and all—but they kept in touch via email and text. It was nice to be able to spend some time together.

Parker blew out a sigh. "Not yet. Still up in the air."

"Shit, Parker. If you don't get it, it may be time to think about jumping ship."

He held back his cringe, but barely. His job, this firm, was everything. His whole life. It was his anchor, his *something*. Something that made him…somebody. The thought of walking away gave him chills. The thought of Nate getting the primo corner office gave him the chills too.

It was a relief when Ash turned to Devlin, asking him about his blog. Because Devlin could talk forever about his blog, releasing Parker from Ash's scrutiny and the need to chat.

Not that small talk didn't have its place, but the headache that had been prowling after him all day was sinking in sharp claws and the whiskey did nothing but make his brain fuzzy. His neurologist had given him pills to take, to quiet his nerves, so the pain wouldn't get too bad, but he hated the pills. He'd rather deal with the pain, when it came, than be muddled all the time.

He couldn't afford muddled.

But the whiskey had muddled his brain too. Must have. His thoughts kept circling around to that woman, the one from the ferry. Something about her—her elfin features, her tight curves, her wide emerald eyes—something had snagged him by the balls and wouldn't let go.

Just thinking about her, here and now in the crowded bar, and his cock stirred.

That was probably why it pole axed him when the front door opened and *she* walked in, as though he'd conjured her with his roiling fantasies. "Oh shit. There she fucking is," he breathed. He didn't mean to say it aloud. The words escaped of their own accord.

Richie glanced at the group of women who had just arrived. "Damn," he muttered. "She is fine. I talked to her on the ferry." He shot a cocky look around the table. "She wants me. She is so fucking hot. I do dig a redhead."

Parker glared at him. Wanted to rip out his throat.

He'd talked to her.

Something that felt like jealousy snarled in his gut. The ache in his neck pinged. He rubbed it, though it didn't help.

"Okay. Yeah. I could fuck that," Devlin said.

Parker's heated gaze swung to the left. Bile rose in his throat. The urge to pummel Devlin's handsome face into mush possessed him.

"The redhead?" Ash asked.

"No. The hottie with the ponytail."

Parker relaxed. Why he relaxed, he didn't know. Didn't know why he'd gone all tense either. He had no claim on her, the redhead. No claim at all. And he didn't want one.

"I could so yank on that." Richie wiped his lip on his sleeve.

A scuffle ensued between Richie and Devlin over who got to claim the woman neither of them had met. The conversation continued, a low drone in Parker's head, but he wasn't listening. His attention was snared. On her. The angle of her head. That hint of a smile. The flutter of her hand.

He really shouldn't have had so much to drink.

When the redhead and her friends finished eating and left the bar, a little bit of light went out of the room.

Which was stupid.

She was just a woman.

Not some kind of angel.

Although, she did look like one—

Yeah. He scuttled that thought too.

After they ate, Ash went back to the house, but the others didn't feel like leaving and stayed at the bar. It was still early evening. No reason to break it up just yet. Although Parker did worry a bit about Richie, who was roaring drunk.

He didn't worry about Richie being roaring drunk as much as he worried about the prospect of having to drag him back home later. Of course, if he collapsed on the floor of the bar, they could probably just let him sleep it off there.

Devlin suggested a game of pool, and they co-opted a table near the back and set up a game. It quickly became clear Richie was in no condition to wield a cue—in fact, he was dangerous with one—so they sat him at the table with a pitcher and played amongst themselves.

Parker missed his shot when the door swung open and she walked back in. He only caught a glimpse of her, out of the corner of his eye, but that was enough. His attention on the game evaporated.

He wasn't the only one who noticed her. Male heads turned as she and her friend—the one with the long ponytail—made their way to the bar. His pulse kicked up a notch. Acid curled in his belly as a couple of peckerwoods zeroed in on them.

Why he felt protective, possessive, of her, he didn't know.

She was just a chick.

A beautiful chick, one whose every movement was like a lyrical poem. One whose face and form made him weak at the knees.

Shit. He focused on the table, though it wasn't his shot, and attempted to thrust her from his mind.

He was far from a monk, but he was careful with women. He had to be. For one thing, in his business, he'd learned they were all pretty shady. And for another—his experience with that species had not been awesome. Oh, it always started out great…until they learned the truth about him.

He'd never forget the look on Chandra's face when—

He pushed the memory away. It was pointless to dwell on things one could not change. It was pointless to think about *this* woman too. A woman like that would get a glimpse of his scars and run for the hills.

Devlin whistled as he chalked his cue. "She's back. Damn, that is a fine piece of ass." Parker was annoyed, until he realized Dev was referring to the brunette with the ponytail. "Maybe we should go rescue them." Because the two women were now surrounded by a herd of salivating lotharios. They should have known better than to come to the bar alone on a Friday night. They should have known they'd be deluged by hot and horny guys.

But, it appeared, these princesses didn't need rescuing. They extricated themselves from the throng and, with a pitcher in hand, made their way to an empty table.

Determinedly, Parker forced his focus back to the game.

For some reason, despite his resolve, it kept drifting back to a minxish redhead with a dazzling smile.

The one who wasn't for him.

Damn.

Damn, damn, damn.

As they wound through the crowd to the empty table, Kaitlin's pulse pounded. She'd come back to the bar with Tara for two reasons. First of all, she didn't want Tara to come alone. And also, she had hoped *he* would still be here.

For some reason, she wanted, very badly to see him again.

And he was. He was over there, in the back, playing pool with Devlin. She took a sip of her beer and studied the crowd, doggedly keeping her gaze off Parker. It took some effort. Her attention kept stalling on him. There was nothing else in the bar as interesting as his long, lean form, his chiseled face, or the vision of his arms bunching as he sighted a shot.

Now that she was over the shock of seeing him again, now that she'd had a little time to process it, she could appreciate the beauty of his aura. Oh, everyone had a beautiful aura. Well, most people. But there was something about his that kept snagging her eye. The bright shimmering lights, the eddy of muted colors, some enigmatic sparkle. It was like staring at diamonds. Or the light when it hit the water on a sunny day. Or a perfect sunrise in a clear sky.

She could stare at him all night.

But she didn't.

She tried not to, at least.

Tara sent her a wicked grin as she refilled her glass. Her colors took on a smoky hue. Kaitlin nibbled her lip as trepidation skirled through her. She wasn't stupid. Though Tara had cheerily suggested they return to the bar for a drink, Kaitlin knew the truth. She knew why her friend had been so adamant about coming back. She had revenge on her mind. It was plastered all over her like a neon sign.

Kaitlin sighed. "Don't do it, Tara."

Thick lashes fluttered. "Don't do what?"

"You know what I mean."

Tara did know. But her truculent expression made it clear. Nothing Kaitlin said or did would change her mind.

Typical.

Though foreboding thrummed in her veins, she knew she couldn't force Tara to give up her plans of revenge—whatever they were. All she could do was be here to pick up the pieces and protect her friend from trouble where she could.

The two men had finished their game of pool and were threading back to their table. Parker took his seat and poured himself another beer as Devlin headed back to the bar.

Poor guy.

He had no idea what was coming.

The vibe Devlin exuded was nice, comfortable, pleasant. Kaitlin hoped he was a forgiving sort, because Tara's energy—not so pleasant. Indeed, it flared as she sprang to her feet and said, in a too-cheerful voice, "I'll be right back."

"Tara…"

She stopped and shot a look over her shoulder. One that made Kaitlin wince.

"Just…be good." It was all she could ask.

Tara's grin was fiendish. "Oh, I will be," she purred.

Kaitlin drew in a deep breath and sent a protective cloak to both Tara and Devlin as her friend sidled up next to him at the bar. The message she got back from the universe stunned her. Amusement, and warmth, rose up in her. Her lips curled.

The next time she glanced up, both Tara and Devlin were gone. Kaitlin sipped her beer as she waited for her friend to return. She didn't drink much as a rule—it blinded her to the insights she relied on, and beer was far from her favorite thing to sip. But it was Friday. And she was on a mini vacation from her life. And she was in a bar.

She checked her watch and frowned when Tara didn't return after a while.

She didn't like being all alone in a room crowded with men. All kinds of sexual innuendoes and predatory energies assaulted her. It brought back bad memories. She did what she always did. Stiffened her spine and surrounded herself with her psychic bands, repelling attention. If that didn't work, a cold, dismissive stare did.

Aside from all that, there was no one to talk to, nothing to take her mind off her worries.

For one thing, she was deeply concerned for her new client, Susan. Susan and her daughter Lily had come into the shelter, covered with bruises—both of them—begging for a safe place to stay. With one touch, Kaitlin had seen it all. She shuddered as the vestigial trails of the memory lashed her.

Poor Susan. She'd known a life of abundance and happiness. Never had to deal with the darker side of the world. And then she'd married Brace. The man of her dreams. It hadn't taken long for him to become the creature of her nightmares.

The abuse from her husband, a man who had vowed to honor and protect her, had deeply scored her soul. And the horror her little girl had suffered at his hands—as the little mite had assumed the weight of his fury when Susan was too beaten to fight back—had wounded her even more.

Kaitlin had taken her pain, spiritual and physical, as much as she could stand. But Susan's well ran deep. It would be a long time, a lot of suffering for all of them, before she could be whole again.

But at least Susan and her daughter had found Boudicca, a well-hidden network of shelters for battered women. They'd be safe there.

A tingling snaked up Kaitlin's spine and she glanced up. Her gaze snagged with that of the Ascot Man, the guy from the ferry who had cornered her in the hall. Though he was here with Devlin and Parker, he stood apart from them, leaning against the wall with his arms crossed, ogling her. His hue was bright red, like fire, with flecks of white. She sent him a cold, dismissive stare. It didn't work. Deliberately, she turned away, scanning the crowd.

Where was Tara? She should have returned by now.

With a gust, Kaitlin stood and made her way to the back of the bar, where her instincts told her Tara had gone. She checked in the ladies room and listened at the door of the men's room—just in case—but there was no one. Nothing. The only other doors were the one to the broom closet—also empty—and the rear exit.

She pushed open the door and the brine-scented breeze teased her nostrils. With it, a hint of Tara's perfume. She'd come out here.

Kaitlin stepped into the shadows and let the door close behind her, and then closed her eyes and trained her attention on the patterns swirling around her.

The taste of old beer and rotting trash from the dumpster filled her senses and she dismissed it. A small critter, scurrying through the gloom—also not what she was looking for.

And then she caught it. A tendril of Tara. Tara twined with a male energy. Devlin. Tara kissing him, teasing him. Rising lust. And—

Oh Tara!

Some mix of dismay and amusement rushed through her as she realized what had happened here. And that Tara had taken what she wanted, and left. Returned to the house, clutching her trophy.

Good gravy. She could have said something. Now Kaitlin would have to make her way back to the house alo—

A sound. A movement. A new presence buffeted her.

She'd been so focused on her hunt, she hadn't realized she was no longer alone.

With a gasp, she whirled to face this threat. But she knew who she'd see. She'd recognized his psychic odor.

He laughed and stepped out of the shadows, the disturbing guy with the ascot, now askew. The sound skittered on the breeze, low and malevolent. He stumbled a bit as the door closed behind him. "Well, well, well," he murmured. "What have we here?"

A memory swamped her. Clawing hands. Hot, wet mouths. Grasping fingers. Sizzling pain. Panic. Her lungs seized and she fought for breath. It came out in short pants. Her skin went cold, then hot, then clammy. She took a step back and scanned the dingy alley for a weapon.

She'd taken self defense classes after that dreadful experience in college, but she was very small and he was large. And he was drunk and he had the vigor of a rampant bull. A horny bull. Quickly, she reviewed her options.

Thumbs to the eyes.

Heel of the palm to the throat.

Knee to the groin.

He lunged.

She danced away, but blinded by her terror, she banged into the hard metal dumpster. A sharp twinge shot through her wrist and she cried out. She whirled to the left. If she could get into the open alley, she could run. He was drunk and he was big and lumbering. She could outrun him.

But before she could sprint, his hands closed harshly on her arm, and he yanked her around. His eyes, already piggy, narrowed even more. His damp, thick lips curled. "Come here," he growled.

She didn't. She fought him, a wild thing, scratching and clawing and thrashing in his hold. His grip tightened. He snarled and flung her around, slamming her into the brick wall of the bar.

She hit hard, and the blow stunned her. She wheezed and struggled for breath, overcome with the pain—the pain of the impact yes, but the pain of his touch as well.

It was always like this when men touched her. Screaming agony as their thoughts, their memories, their intentions clogged her senses. It was too much. Too much. She couldn't. She couldn't—

And then—*ah, God*—he whipped her around and pushed up against her fully, sealing them together from chest to groin. The sour stench of his breath and his sweat surrounded her like a cloud. His heat singed her. He pinned her to the cold, hard wall, grabbed her breast, and squeezed.

"No," she cried. *No!*

"Shut up," he snarled, fiddling between them. With horror she realized he was unsnapping her jeans.

Her knee jerked up but she hit his thigh and he laughed, a low chuckle. "Oh, yeah," he whispered, a pernicious rush. "I like a fighter."

He was utterly focused on her. He didn't hear the door open. Didn't feel the ferocious force swelling up behind him. Didn't taste the danger.

She did.

She steeled herself for the onslaught.

"Leave her alone," an incensed voice snarled.

It washed through her consciousness, percolating to the depths of her memory, scudding back to *that night*. She remembered his voice, of course. Though she'd only heard him say three words. Just those three words, growled in a dark tone. Burned on her memory.

Leave her alone.

He'd saved her that long ago night with those three words—saved her from God knows what. The boys in that back room had taken one glance at him and scattered.

He'd saved her that night, and he would save her again.

Hard hands ripped her assailant away and spun him around. A fist to the gut landed with a heavy thud. A grunt. A wheeze. The rampant bull deflated, dropped to his knees and then collapsed on the filthy cement.

Parker stood over him, his fists on his hips, his features tight. "Goddamn it, Richie," he muttered. And then he turned to Kaitlin. Held out a hand. "Are you all right?"

She opened her mouth to respond, but couldn't. Her muscles locked. Her body shook. She teetered, but he caught her.

The familiar pain engulfed her at his touch, burned through her soul as she tasted his darkness. But then it changed. Warmed. Became something else. Something, gentle and sweet.

She nestled into his arms, relieved when he wrapped them around her like a blanket.

Oh, what heaven, the luxury of a touch after a lifetime of denial. She searched for discomfort. There was none. Well, there was some discomfort, but it was different. A dull ache...for more. Hunger, perhaps.

The realization stunned her. She stared up at him in wonder. His face was, as she remembered it, painfully handsome. Sharp features and wide gray eyes. His cheeks were high, his lips beautifully shaped and his nose, a strong blade. There was a U-shaped scar on his left cheek. His chin was square and had an off-center dent. His shoulders were broad and his neck muscled. A birthmark rose on the left side of it, above the neck of his shirt. And heavens, he was tall.

"Are you okay?" he repeated.

She nodded, a jerky bob of her head, but clung to him. He was so...*comfortable*.

"Are you sure?"

"Yes." Oh yes. She'd never *felt* better.

CHAPTER THREE

Shit.

Parker's hand hurt like hell. But goddamn Richie. Goddamn him for what he'd done. He'd scared her half to death. When she looked up at him, her eyes wide and filled with tears, he wanted to storm over there and pound on him some more.

She was fragile, tiny and shivering with reaction. It made his heart ache. It reminded him of another woman. Slight and defenseless against a brawny man's meaty fists—

Fucking Asshole. Yeah, he was drunk. But that was no fucking excuse for this.

He tightened his hold on her, ignoring how right it felt having her in his arms. His headache had disappeared altogether—probably the aftereffect of the adrenaline coursing through his system at the sight of Richie pinning this woman against the wall and mauling her. *His* woman. His—

Shit. She wasn't his. Wasn't his anything.

But she was shaken, possibly in shock. He couldn't just leave her here alone. "Let me walk you home," he said.

Her head snapped up. Her lips parted. He was possessed of the crazy urge to cover them with his. To soothe her, comfort her with his body. He thrust it away.

No. He'd already decided this was the kind of woman he needed to avoid. Besides which, the last thing she'd want right now was some other man assaulting her. Gently, resolutely, he set her back, waiting until she found her balance before releasing her.

"You-you don't have to do that. I can go myself."

Everything in him quailed at her rebuff. First, he didn't want to let her go. On the most basic level he couldn't tolerate the thought of watching her walk away. Second of all, she was still trembling like a leaf. It wouldn't be right to just leave her here.

"It's okay." He cleared his throat as something rose up to clog it. "I won't hurt you."

Her eyes widened and she snorted something that might have been a laugh.

"I'm Parker." He thrust out a hand. A friendly gesture. Perhaps the incongruous normality of it would convince her to trust him.

She stared at his hand. He was certain she was going to ignore it when slowly, she slipped hers into his. The rush of elation at that simple touch, two palms kissing, was devastating. And absurd.

It was just a fleeting touch. It should not feel so good. Should not fill him, body and soul with such…peace.

But it did.

"I'm Kaitlin," she whispered. Her voice was melodic, as lyrical as the rest of her. She seemed not of this world in that moment, like a mythological creature come to life. A siren perhaps.

Kaitlin.

He pressed back the urge to kiss her as it rose once more.

"Let me walk you home."

"I'm sure it's fine now." She glanced down at Richie's groaning form.

Parker hadn't hit him that hard; it was probably the alcohol that had done him in. "Of course it is. But I won't rest tonight until I know you are home safe." He held out an arm, like a gentleman of old—which was ridiculous because there was not an ounce of chivalry in his makeup. He was a divorce attorney, for Christ's sake.

He ignored the gratification rushing through him when she set her hand on his arm and followed him back into the bar. The noise of the place slammed into him and he winced. It hadn't bothered him before, but this altercation with Richie had frazzled his nerves. He noticed she winced too, so he put his arm around her slight shoulders, reveling in how damn good that felt, and headed for the door.

He paused as he came even with the waitress and tipped his head toward the back door. "There's a mess out there," he said.

She rolled her eyes and muttered, "Not again."

"You'd…better send Darby," he suggested with a meaningful look. She glanced at Kaitlin, who was still shaken, and nodded, heading for the beefy bartender. Darby didn't take shit from anyone; he'd probably been in a brawl or two in his life. No doubt he was used to managing recalcitrant drunks.

Without further delay, Parker whisked Kaitlin from the premises.

The cool evening breeze was a balm as they stepped out into the night. "How are you doing?" he asked when she stumbled.

She cleared her throat. "I'm fine. Thank you." She stopped, suddenly, and turned to face him. Something within him ached when she pulled out of his arms, but her eyes were limpid, gorgeous, glinting in the moonlight. He could swim in them. "I mean, *thank you*."

Heat crawled up Parker's neck. Part of it was a discomfiting wash of bashfulness at the way she gazed at him, as though he were some kind of hero. He wasn't. But part of it was the gut-churning horror at what could have happened if he hadn't had the odd compulsion to follow Richie out to the back. "No worries," he muttered. "So, where are you staying?"

She pointed to the north, toward the houses along the beach. He nodded and took her arm again and together they strolled up the path. They didn't speak as they walked. Indeed, Parker couldn't think of anything to say, which was totally contrary to his nature. He was used to coming up with slick words for every circumstance; uncomfortable situations were his forte.

But the moment didn't seem to call for small talk. And oddly enough, *they* didn't require it. She stumbled again when they hit a shadowy part of the path and he grabbed for her hand. She froze for a second or two, and then twined her fingers through his.

Funny. They walked like that. Holding hands. Like lovers. Or something.

He pushed the thought away.

They came to Ash's house and he followed her lead, to the next house, another one of the large mansions along the road. She stopped.

"This is it," she said.

Great. He could spend the rest of the night lying awake in his bed, suffused with the knowledge that she was right next door.

"Okay." How he got the word out, he didn't know.

She peeped up at him through her lashes and it hit him again, how goddamn beautiful she was.

"Thank you again," she whispered, stepping close. Too close. Her scent engulfed him. Her warmth enrobed him. She set her palm on his chest and leaned in and then—*God Almighty*—pressed her lips to his. Just to the corner of his mouth, not a real kiss at all.

It slammed through him like a fist to the gut.

Instinct took over.

Damn instinct.

He cupped her cheeks and held her there, then tipped his head, just a bit, and sealed his mouth over hers.

Jesus. She tasted sweet. So sweet.

It wasn't a passionate kiss. No sucking or tangling tongues. No rabid passion. No *thrusting.* Just a tender touch of lips. He couldn't bear to step away. If she hadn't, he'd probably have remained there, in that embrace, all night.

Though she ended the kiss, her palm remained on his chest for a long while as she gazed into his eyes.

He thought, perhaps, she might kiss him again. Indeed, she swayed closer. Her lips parted. A cricket chirruped to his left. The moment swelled between them.

But then the screen door of her house slammed open.

"Hey, Kait?" A low booming voice shattered the fragile web. "Is that you?"

She leaped away and glanced over her shoulder. "Hey, Drew," she called. "I'll be right in." She shot Parker a crooked smile. It skewered him. "Thank you again," she said. And then she left.

He watched her climb the stairs and greet the muscular man at the door with a nod. He glared at Parker over her head and then, with sharp movements, pulled her inside and shut the door with a decisive click.

Parker stared at the place she'd been. He should probably leave. Make his way back to Ash's house and throw himself into bed and work on wiping her from his mind.

But he couldn't.

She was stuck in there. In his mind. In his veins. In his soul.

Damn.

* * *

"Who was that douche canoe?" Drew asked as he herded Kaitlin down the hall into the great room where the others were assembled playing a game of Movie Charades. She barely heard him. Her mind was spinning, her body still shaking a bit with reaction. Odd that it was more of a response to that kiss, than to the attack. Her muscles tightened as she thought of *that*.

She couldn't tell Drew what had happened behind that bar. She couldn't tell any of them. The guys would go ballistic.

She called down a white light and allowed it to soothe her. It helped that she saw Tara sitting, calm as you please on a stool at the kitchen counter. Though annoyance trickled through her, she let out a breath. It was a relief to see her safe, especially after the emotional upheaval Kaitlin had been through tonight—

"Hello? Kait? Who was he?"

"That was Parker," she said, ducking into the kitchen to find her stash of chocolate. "He walked me home."

Drew's brow rumpled. "Walked you home?"

"From Darby's."

His frown became a glower. Drew was like a guard dog sometimes. A guard dog with a bone. That needed guarding. "What were you doing at Darby's alone?"

Kaitlin blew out a snort and popped a square of chocolate into her mouth. "I wasn't alone."

Tara caught her eye and winced, mouthing, "Sorry."

"You should have texted me. I would have come and got you."

"Honestly, Drew. I'm fine. Besides, I didn't know you were here. When did you get in?"

He stilled. "Well, just a few minutes ago, but that's beside the point."

She patted him on the arm and moved out of his embrace. It was unnerving, and he had the tendency to cling. She walked to the fridge, though she wasn't hungry, opened it and stared inside.

"Can I make you a sandwich?" he asked.

She closed the door. "No. I'm not hungry." She glanced around the room. "Where are Jamie and Emily?"

Drew shrugged. "They went to bed, I guess. Do you want to play pool?"

There was a table downstairs. But he didn't want to play pool. He wanted to spend time alone with her. That was never wise. Besides, pool made her think of Parker again.

"No. Thanks." She shot him a smile, which he returned. He was so handsome. Adorable, really. And he was such a sweet soul. She wished she could return his feelings—she was so tired of being alone—but she couldn't. She just couldn't.

A sudden exhaustion swamped her and she yawned. She should go upstairs and tuck in, but she knew if she tried to sleep now, memories of her recent ordeal would surround her like a thick cloak. Instead, she threw herself on the sofa between Holt and Kristi and nibbled more chocolate as she watched Cam act out a the title of a movie while everyone tried to guess what it was. Drew sat on the other sofa and stared at her.

The charades were hysterical. Or, at least Kaitlin assumed as much, judging from all the laughter. She wasn't really paying attention. She was working on her calm, calling on her spirit guides, marshalling that psychic wall she relied on to protect her from a buffeting emotional storm.

It helped to be surrounded by friends, all of them with positive, healing energy. And after a while, she found herself laughing too as Bella tried to convey *Twelve Monkeys*, hooting and scratching her pits.

Kaitlin knew—*knew*—it was *Twelve Monkeys*, so she didn't guess. She never guessed. It wasn't fair and it was far too much fun watching the others try to figure it out. Besides, the person who guessed correctly had to go next. If Kaitlin guessed, she would get it right; it would always be her turn. And that would be exhausting.

"Um...*Planet of the Apes?*" Cam guessed. Bella shook her head.

"*2001: A Space Odyssey*," Kristi crowed. Bella frowned at her and went into conniptions again.

"*9 ½ Weeks.*" This from Holt. Everyone groaned. Holt always guessed *9 ½ Weeks*. No matter what.

Bella propped her hands on her hips. "At least *try* to pay attention," she muttered.

"I am paying attention," Holt said with a smirk. The message that passed between him and Bella sizzled. Kaitlin was surprised no one else caught it. You didn't have to have psychic energies to feel the heat scouring the room between them.

Holt's arousal swelled. Kaitlin shot him a look. She didn't mean to, it just happened. He caught her eye and stilled. A flush rose on his cheeks. And then he laughed. "Sorry," he murmured.

She patted him on the arm. "Just try not to leap on her until you're private," she whispered. She loved that her friends knew her and accepted her as she was. They weren't freaked out, like so many people were, when she read their secrets as though they wore them on sandwich boards.

Holt chuckled. "I'll try." He reached an arm behind her, draping it over the back of the couch, but didn't touch her. They all knew how uncomfortable it made her to be touched and were always careful. All but Drew, who sometimes forgot. He tried to remember, though, and she appreciated that.

How odd that it hadn't hurt when Parker had held her. There had been that first moment of discomfort, but she hadn't felt it again. And when she'd kissed him...when he'd kissed her, there had been nothing but pleasure.

Astonishing.

His mouth had been on hers. Covering hers. She hadn't felt a raging agony. There had been no flail of panic. No suffocating sensation.

Just the flash of excitement and...a hunger for more.

Drew, who was watching her with a simmering focus, frowned and said in an overloud voice, "I give up Bella. Kaitlin, what is it?"

Everyone turned to her expectantly. She sighed and stored all thoughts of Parker away...for later. "*Twelve Monkeys.*"

"Yes!" Bella crowed tapping her nose. "You got it! Your turn."

"But I don't want to—"

Bella grabbed her arm and pulled her off the couch and into the middle of the room. "You have to. It's the rules."

"I hate this game." And not only because she sucked at it. She hated when people gawked at her. Even if they were her friends.

But fate was with her. She reached into the bowl and pulled out a slip of paper. Read it and fell to the ground in an overblown death scene.

"*Die Hard!*" Drew bellowed as he leaped to his feet.

"No fair!" Kristi cried. "That was an easy one."

Kaitlin sat up and grinned at her. "It was in the bowl."

"No fair!" But Kristi couldn't hold back her smile.

The game continued on with Drew and then Tara and then Bella again taking a turn. Kaitlin joined in the fun, laughing and joking—and not guessing. And not taking the lead again.

She simply leaned back on the couch and soaked it in. This circle of friends, their ridiculous antics. Their friendship and love. She let it slip into her and suffuse her and remind her of all the good in the world.

CHAPTER FOUR

She woke up at dawn, though she hadn't slept very well, with a sudden urge to walk on the beach. Tiptoeing around the room so she wouldn't wake Jamie, she found shorts, a tee shirt and windbreaker, and then stepped into her flip flops and eased into the hall.

The house was quiet. As she came down the stairs the first rays of dawn were lightening the water. She flicked on the coffee maker so it would be ready by the time she got back, or if anyone else woke up, and she opened the slider.

She loved the dawn. Such a peaceful time of day. The birds in the trees were just starting to chirp and the breeze was still cool and kissed with the mists of night. She drew in a deep breath as she made her way down the steps to the beach and then followed the shore toward the point. The damp sand was hard beneath her feet, but if she glanced back she saw the little ponds her footsteps made as the indents filled with water. She wasn't sure why this amused her, but it did.

Little things like that just did.

As she rounded the point, the little island to the northwest came into view, hunkered as it was in trails of fog. It looked lonely and bereft. A shiver walked through her.

She shook the feeling off. Like so many others, it made no sense. She'd always been filled with far-fetched notions. Some of them turned out to *be* something. Others did not. The little island was just an island. The little puddles in the sand were just footprints. There was nothing more to it.

As a girl, Kaitlin had trusted all of her instincts, followed every hunch. As a result, she frequently got into trouble, or annoyed her friends. Occasionally the neighbors. Her mother had told her—more than once—to grow up, that she was fanciful and overdramatic. And Kaitlin had believed her. She'd tried very hard to ignore the whispers—despite her bone-deep conviction they were *real*.

It wasn't until she was twelve, and met her Aunt Cecily, that she learned the truth. "The Gift" ran in the family. Everyone was *touched*, although it had skipped Kaitlin's mother. She'd gone so far as to move herself and Kaitlin to Seattle to get away from "the crazy."

Aunt Cecily had explained everything. She'd helped Kaitlin make sense of the swirling sentiments, the overwhelming onslaughts, the *knowledge*. She'd given her tips and tricks to deal with, what her mother called "her condition."

It had taken years for Kaitlin to come into her own. To be confident and strong. To learn how to use her gift for the best of all. If it hadn't been for Aunt Cecily's guidance, she would probably have been locked in a loony bin long ago. Now she accepted it as a part of herself, even if other people couldn't.

Her mother still avoided her sometimes as though she had a plague.

A movement in the tree line ahead caught her attention and Kaitlin stopped in her tracks. A man wearing a white long-sleeved t-shirt and jeans—despite the fact it was summer—stood there, hands on his hips, staring up into the branches.

She recognized his aura.

How could she not? She'd thought about it all night long.

Timidity swamped her and, for a moment, she considered turning around and heading back to the house, but for some reason, her feet moved her toward him.

Oh, she knew the reason. She was drawn to him. In a way she'd never experienced before. Like filings to a magnet. And she wanted, ached, to *be* with him again.

He turned as she approached, and then did a double take.

"Oh. Hi, Kaitlin," he said.

"Good morning, Parker." She tipped up her head. "What's up there?"

He frowned. "Some idiot flew a kite and the strings got tangled in the limbs. And they left it there." He peered up into the rustling branches. "Something's caught. I think it's an eagle."

Kaitlin's heart lurched. She reached out and felt the energy. *Fear. Pain. Panic.* And yes. It was an eagle. "We must free it."

He nodded. "That's what I was thinking. I have a Swiss army knife," he pulled it out of his pocket and cradled it in his palm. "But if I climb up there to cut it loose, I'm afraid I might hurt it more as it tries to escape."

She took off her jacket. "Wrap it in this and be sure to cover its eyes. It may not work, but birds usually calm when they cannot see. Then cut the main lines holding it and carry it down. We can remove all the string and hopefully, it's not too injured to fly."

He met her gaze. "Good idea. Is there a Waystation around here, in case it's hurt?"

Kaitlin shook her head. "There's one on the mainland."

"Well, fingers crossed then." He took her jacket and slung it over his shoulder then opened the knife and gripped it with his teeth.

Kaitlin watched, her pulse thudding in her throat as he climbed high into the branches. As he neared, the eagle began to thrash. Kaitlin tried to send it calming waves.

Several grunts and curses wafted through the boughs, and then snaps and cracks as Parker made his way down the tree. "I got him," he called as he reached the bottom with the eagle swathed in her jacket.

He shouldn't have called.

The raptor began to thrash again and a talon swiped out and caught Parker across his abdomen.

He hissed as a long red stain appeared on his shirt, but to his credit, he didn't lose hold of the bird. Kaitlin ran forward to help.

"Stay back," he hissed. "You'll get hurt."

"I won't get hurt," she said, grasping the exposed talon with one hand and setting her hand on the body of the bird, whispering to it. It continued to fight for a moment, and then settled.

"How did you do that?" Parker asked.

Kaitlin just smiled. "Lay him on the sand. Let's cut him free." She could see how tightly the string bound the poor creature. It must have been struggling for hours.

"I dropped the knife," Parker said nodding his head toward the tree.

"I'll get it." Kaitlin leaped up and ran for the base of the tree, quickly finding the red knife against the brown pine needles. She pulled out the tiny scissors as she hurried back. "Hold him still while I cut him free."

Parker grunted as a talon flashed again catching him on the sleeve of his shirt.

"He's just frightened," she said in a lulling tone as she began to snip the lines. "Nothing to be afraid of here, little eagle. We're here to help you. We're not going to hurt you. No. We're not."

She focused on calming the bird as she worked, pouring all her concentration into the task, gratified that the creature seemed to understand she was trying to save it.

She was amazing.

Parker watched her as she worked. Not her fingers, her face. Her entire countenance was imbued with light, with a serene, soothing confidence. The bird felt it. He certainly did as well.

Her coos reminded him of a lullaby from long ago, so long ago it was swamped in darkness, but somehow, it shone through.

He held the eagle as still as he could as she worked, all the while entranced by the spell she was weaving over the bird. Over them both.

As she cut away the string, being careful not to snip a feather, she peeled back the jacket until she reached the head. With a sigh, she snipped the last line.

The raptor observed her with unblinking eyes, surreally relaxed, as though it understood. It was a magnificent animal with thick muscled shoulders and legs and a wicked hooked beak.

"Okay now. I'm done. I got it all. Ease the jacket away and let him try to stand."

Parker did so, ready to make a grab for the bird if it suddenly attacked. It was large enough to do serious damage to an alabaster face. Kaitlin seemed to have no fear. She cooed again, encouraging it to struggle to its feet. It took one step, two, then spread its wings. It flapped once and then, with a small hop, took off in a great whoosh, soaring into the sky, letting out a gleeful cry.

She stared after it, her eyes wide, lips parted.

He'd never seen anything more magnificent.

Her face, that was. His attention was locked on it.

"You were wonderful," he said.

She laughed. "You were. Climbing up that tree... Capturing the bird. Bringing it back down without hurting it, even though it was struggling..."

Their gazes tangled.

For some reason, he was suffused in the memory of last night's kiss, though in truth, it had never been far from his mind.

His ardor rose.

He wanted to kiss her again. Here. Now.

Wanted more, perhaps.

She looked away, as though the intensity between them was too strong. Her focus snagged on his shirt. Her eyes went wide. "You're hurt."

He glanced down. Yeah, it was pretty bad.

"Let me see." She tugged at his shirt, lifting it.

No! A voice screamed in his head. *Don't let her see.* Parker lurched back, out of reach. "It's nothing."

She frowned at him. "It's not nothing. And there's another cut on your arm."

Yeah. He felt that one, a throbbing ache. As pain went, it wasn't too bad. "It's okay." He stood and teetered a little as his head went light. She was there by his side in a heartbeat, looping her arm around his waist so she could help him walk.

What a joke. She was the tiniest thing he'd ever seen. If he fell, there was no way she could stop it.

But he let her help him. Because he couldn't bear to refuse. It felt too good, touching her again. They made their way back to Ash's house on the wet sand at the surf line because it made walking easier. When they got to her place, she turned to head up the stairs, but he stopped. She peered up at him. "Here?"

He shook his head and pointed to the house next door. "I'm over here."

She nodded, as though she understood his need to be in a familiar place, and allowed him to guide her to the basement door. He was glad he'd taken that room, especially now. The stairs up to the main deck seemed like the slopes of Kilimanjaro. Though it hadn't hurt so much on the beach, the cut to his abdomen was really starting to sting and the blood stain was becoming alarming.

The bottom floor of Ash's place was a daylight basement that stretched the breadth of the house, though not much daylight seeped in. But there was enough to see, as Parker made his way across the room to the bedroom in the corner. He flicked on the light and collapsed on the bed. *Damn.* That did hurt.

"First aid kit?" she asked in a no nonsense voice.

"In the bathroom. Under the sink." He nodded in that direction.

When she took off to find it, he carefully peeled back his shirt and frowned. The cut was nasty, but not too deep. He wouldn't need stitches, but it would have to be wrapped and he'd probably need to go see Doctor Marks first thing on Monday. Maybe get a rabies shot or something.

A gasp from the doorway shot through him like a bullet. He yanked his shirt down but it was too late; he could tell by the expression on her face, she'd seen. "It's not bad," he said in a light voice.

She snorted and dumped gauze, peroxide, antiseptic and tape on the bed.

And then she dropped to her knees before him.

Holy Jesus God. She dropped to her knees before him. In his bedroom.

A devastating lust swept away the mortification that she'd seen his scars. He nearly lost consciousness. Despite the fact he was in pain, his cock rose.

What was it about this woman?

On her knees before him?

"It needs tending," she said, ripping open a package of gauze and setting it aside. "Lift your shirt."

He cringed.

Lift his shirt?

On purpose?

In front of a woman?

A woman he wanted to—

"Lift. Your. Shirt." Her tone brooked no refusal.

"Kaitlin..." He should warn her. She'd seen it, but maybe she hadn't *really* seen it.

"Parker, I need to get some peroxide on it and quickly. Please. Lift your shirt."

Well hell.

It had been a nice fantasy, while it lasted. Once she saw, she'd run screeching the other way. They all did. Or, if they didn't screech, their noses would curl up and their faces would go all cold. And then they'd *quietly* run away.

Slowly, he pulled up the hem.

And hell. Yes. Her nose wrinkled.

But she didn't run.

She touched him. She touched his scars—mottled and discolored and ugly—thumbing them gently. "Hmm," she said, turning away to open the bottle of hydrogen peroxide and soaking the gauze with it. She met his gaze saying, "This will be cold," before daubing it on his cut.

He flinched when she touched him.

"Sorry," she muttered. "Did that hurt?"

"No." It didn't hurt. But then, it wouldn't.

Most of the nerves there were dead. The only place it burned was on the sides, where his scars weren't quite so thick.

She gently dabbed at him, making sure to get the antiseptic over the whole cut. "I'm going to cover this, but I need to wrap it around your waist," she said. "It will be easier if you take off your shirt."

God. No.

His belly was bad enough. But the rest of him?

"Kaitlin…"

"I need to do your arm too."

"I can do my arm."

She sent him a mocking pout. "Parker, let me help you. You helped me last night. It would be my honor to return the favor."

God bless her. She was so damn sincere and genuine. How could he explain?

"I don't like taking off my shirt," he said. Well, that didn't explain much. Then again, it explained everything. "These scars…" He waved to his exposed stomach. Hell he could barely stand to look at it himself. He hated the way he looked. Had since he was five.

"Yes?"

He sucked in a breath, steeling his spine. "I have them…all over."

She set her hand on his knee. Her jaw went slack. Her eyes glazed over. "Wow," she said after a long moment. She cleared her throat. "That must have hurt a lot."

He cracked a grin. He did not know why. "Yes. Yes it did."

"Okay. Now take off your shirt."

"Kaitlin…"

"Just do it, Parker. Let me wrap this up and then you can put your armor back on." This she said gently, with no discernible derision. It was horrifying how she seemed to see right through to his soul. Then again, it was comforting as well.

Which was probably why he did it…why he took the hem of his shirt in his hands and pulled it off. Exposing himself to another human—not in the medical profession—for the first time in years.

CHAPTER FIVE

Kaitlin forced her features into a blasé moue and got to work wrapping the long gauze around Parker's abdomen, holding the bandage in place. What she'd seen in that moment of time, when he'd stared into her eyes, had devastated her.

Such pain. Such agony.

And the physical pain had been the very least of it. A mere twinge in a sea of anguish.

His chest was, indeed, covered with scars. Old ones and newer ones. She understood now that flicker of pain she'd felt the first time they'd touched. That scorch of flames. He'd been burned, and burned badly. There were thick patches and other, funny colored spots where they'd done grafts. There were long incisions where some other procedures had been done. And God knew what else. One round puckered scar on his chest looked like a bullet wound. Kaitlin couldn't help smoothing her palm over the spots that glowed red in his aura, willing healing energy to seep down deep.

Whatever this was, it had happened long ago, but the pain still lingered.

It was difficult, being so close to him. Each time she wound the gauze around him she had to lean close, almost touching. It wasn't a discomfort she was used to, that prickly sizzle of raw emotion. This was a different kind of sizzle. A craving.

He smelled wonderful, of aftershave and sweat. She wanted to coil herself around him and hold on. But she couldn't. First of all, she needed to finish bandaging him up.

Second of all, she could sense his embarrassment. He was uneasy, being so exposed. As she worked, she sent him reassuring waves and felt his tension relax.

She turned her attention to his arm, quickly cleaning and wrapping that gash. The scars covered his shoulders and traced down to his wrist on one arm and to the elbow on the other. Odd for a burn. As though the fire had been dribbled on him.

"Does it still hurt?" she asked, before she could stop herself.

He froze and glanced away. "Not much."

"Not much?"

His lips tweaked. "Funny thing about burns. If they go deep enough, the nerves get fried too."

"Hmm." What could one say to that? "Lucky you."

He caught her sarcasm and snorted a laugh. Then sobered. "I *was* lucky. They say if the flames had reached my hands or my face, I would probably have died." He held up a broad palm. "More nerves here than on ninety percent of your body." He shrugged. "Or something like that."

"I didn't know that." She quirked a grin. She was done and he wasn't rushing to cover up. That was something. It spoke to his comfort with her, perhaps. She hoped.

"You learn a lot of handy medical tidbits when you spend a chunk of your life as a kid in a burn ward."

"How old were you?" She asked, though she already knew. Young. Too young to suffer through such an experience. And the physical scarring was only the tip of the iceberg.

"Five."

She touched his hand. Not a light touch, but a full, warm clasp. "I am so sorry, Parker."

He shrugged. One shoulder. "Thanks. It's over."

But it wasn't.

It wasn't.

He still carried wounds—and not just those on his skin.

It was as though he stood on a desolate hill, stalwart and brave and absolutely alone. His isolation sheathed him. Caged him.

All of a sudden, she was suffused by the overpowering urge to ease his spirit, to relieve his solitude—if only for a moment. To show him the world was not a bleak wasteland. That he didn't have to travel it alone.

She knew what he wanted. Knew what he needed. She'd tasted his simmering desire. Felt it thrumming on the air.

And she wanted it too.

For the first time in her life, she wanted it too. She ached to taste him.

Slowly, she eased her hand up his thighs, over his hips. And she unsnapped his jeans.

Parker froze. He stared at Kaitlin, this beautiful, incredibly alluring woman as she unfastened his jeans. *Unfastened his jeans.* Lust blazed through him. His pulse pounded painfully. His cock went on point.

Shit.

It had been tormenting, having her lean in, again and again, so close—her scent, her warmth surrounding him like a cloud as she wrapped his injury. He'd fisted the covers to keep from grabbing her and yanking her against him.

And now…this?

He should stop her. That's what he should do. Grab her wrists and still her movements.

But he couldn't.

It had been so long…and damn it, he wanted her.

She glanced up at him, a question in her eyes.

He opened his lips to tell her no, but that word didn't come out. "Kaitlin," he huffed, on a breath.

She took this as assent and stroked his hard length through the cotton. A teasing trail. A shudder rocked him. God, it felt so good. A groan escaped from his throat. She rolled down his briefs. His cock bounded out and he frowned. She was far too delicate for such a rampant—

"Oh my," she said. And she took him in her hands.

His vision blurred as she wrapped him in a warm fist and stroked. Delight danced up his spine.

"Kaitlin…"

She dipped her head and her tongue peeped out. He held his breath as she neared. And *ah!* Bliss as a velvet softness stroked the tip of his cock, licking at the eye, lapping up a bead of cum.

She swirled it around the head and more quakes claimed him. A snarl began at the base of his balls. Hell, he wasn't going to last. He clenched his ass to hold back. Because, God, he wanted to last. He wanted *this* to last.

She murmured something—he had no clue what it was because his ears were filled with the sound of his scudding heartbeat—but the vibration slid through him like a knife of pleasure.

Her lips parted and she drew him in, sucking at the tip as she stroked him gently. She was tentative, untrained, but he didn't care. He couldn't. It was too fucking awesome. Perfect. She explored him with leisurely kisses and caresses, tracing the long bulging vein down to his nest and then nibbling her way back up. Each touch, each lick, each agonizing lap drove him deeper into insanity. But it was a delicious madness.

Edging higher, she took him deeper, burying his cock in her throat. Sensation scored him, his mind spun, his breath wheezed. And she sucked.

"Ah! God." A warble.

Though he filled her mouth, he felt her smile. She began a slow sultry slide. Up and down, up and down. He squeezed his eyes shut and focused on it, taking it all in, memorizing it.

When her haphazard movements became too excruciating to bear, he laced his fingers in her hair and guided her in a more satisfying rhythm. She seemed to understand what he was asking for, because once she caught the pace, *holy fuck*, once she caught the pace, she devastated him.

Moving faster, holding him more firmly, sucking harder, she worked him.

He should stop her, he thought as the snarl in his balls became a howl, when his body constricted and he felt the familiar harbingers of orgasm.

It was wrong to use her like this, to let her please him without giving anything back. To empty himself in her mouth.

But he couldn't stop. Couldn't…

Her fingers fluttered over his thighs, over his belly, over his chest. She set her palms flat on him, this beautiful girl, and stroked his hideous scars—as though she didn't care.

As though she didn't see him as a freak. As ugly. As someone who really didn't belong in this world.

He had yearned for this, yearned for such acceptance, his entire life.

It rose, the demanding beast coiled in his belly. It rose, and roared. Unable to control himself, he held on to the back of her head and thrust into her mouth. She took him. All the way.

Her hands drifted over his mottled skin, finding all his scars and loving them. And then, as though she knew, as though she felt his crisis approach, she encircled him. Intensified her barrage. Coaxed him to detonate.

It was blinding, the bliss. A hot white curtain fell, engulfing him in sensation, in an unaccountable serenity. He shook, lunged, howled as he released.

And she took it all. She took everything.

Without hesitation.

He stared down at her as she continued to suck and swallow and consume his seed, his soul. Her eyes were closed, as though she was soaking it in as well. As though what he'd given her had pleased her.

No one had ever done that for him.

No one had ever accepted who he was—scars and all.

No one had ever embraced him in such a fashion.

When, finally she lifted her head, he yanked her up into his arms and kissed her.

Not the gentle sweet buss from last night. This was a frantic thing, but a thing of desperate thanks.

God help him. She was perfect.

He was lost.

She hadn't expected him to kiss her like that.

Though she could tell from his frenzied reaction to her touch, from his moans and the rise of his root chakra energy, he enjoyed what she'd done. And he'd come. Erupted into her mouth with a flood of salty, musky flavor, tinged as it was, by his pleasure.

It had been delicious.

She'd known she'd pleased him. But she hadn't expected the kiss, the wave of raw gratitude.

When he pulled back, he didn't say anything. He just looked at her with his palm on her cheek, his thumb stroking her lips. His gaze was bold, brash, as though he could see to her soul. A sudden shyness suffused her.

"I..." She began cleaning up the papers and wrappers strewn on the bed. "I should go."

"Kaitlin."

She stilled and met his eyes. "Yes, Parker?"

"Thank you."

Her lips quirked up. "You're welcome."

"No. I mean...*thank you*."

As she gazed at him she saw it. The depth of his appreciation. But she felt it too. For a short while, two very lonely souls hadn't been so very alone.

"Will I see you again?" he asked.

"I'm here all weekend," she murmured. "I hope so. Thank you for saving the eagle."

He gestured at his bandage, or perhaps to his groin. "Thank you for saving me."

She slipped out of the house the same way she'd come in and made her way back home. Astonishingly, no one was up when she pushed through the door. It seemed like a hundred years, a lifetime, had passed since she'd left this morning.

But the coffee was ready. She poured herself a cup and went to sit on the deck and watch the water. She tried to enjoy the view, the breeze, the scent of pine wafting through the boughs, but she couldn't. She was suffused with his scent. It filled her, saturated her.

Her body hummed for completion, pinged with an ache she didn't understand—but did.

After a while Jamie came down the stairs and joined her on the deck, which was nice. The distraction. They chatted about nonsense. Television shows and movies and an art auction she'd gone to recently. When Bella and Holt wandered into the kitchen, she and Jamie went inside and started talking about what they wanted for breakfast. They were debating between French toast and pancakes when Tara padded downstairs with a yawn.

"What do you want for breakfast, Tara?" Bella asked.

Tara snorted. "I am not making breakfast."

"Did I ask you to make breakfast?"

"I know you, Bella. A question like that? In the morning? To a baker? It's my day off."

Bella looked at Holt. "I didn't ask her to *make* breakfast, did I? I simply said, 'What do you *want* for breakfast.' Huge difference."

Holt held up his hands and snorted a laugh. "Leave me out of this."

"It's Emily's turn to cook, anyway," Bella muttered.

Kaitlin frowned as something pinged in the back of her consciousness.

"Is it?" Jamie asked.

"Yeah. The last time we came, Kristi and I cooked."

Tara wrinkled her nose. "I heard you made some weird tofu thing. Surely that doesn't count."

Bella blew out a breath. *"Jeese-o-frickin-peese.* I'm telling you. It's Emily's turn to cook!"

That something pinged again. Kaitlin stilled and tried to focus on it. It grew. Her gut lurched.

Good gravy.

"Where is Emily?" Her tone must have carried her panic because everyone froze and glanced around the room.

"Emily?" Holt scrubbed his face with a palm.

"Still in bed?" Bella muttered.

"Is she?" Kaitlin knew she wasn't, knew Emily was not in this house. And hadn't been for some time.

Why, oh why hadn't she sensed it sooner?

Because she'd been distracted that's why. She'd been too focused on herself. Heat crawled up her neck. A prickle of dread blossomed as Bella stomped upstairs to check on Emily. She returned, subdued. "Emily's not there. And her bed hasn't been slept in."

"When is that last time anyone saw her?" Holt asked.

Bella tapped her lip. "Last night."

Jamie nodded. "She came back from Darby's with us."

"And no one saw her leave after that?" Kaitlin wandered to the slider and stared out at the ocean. It was calm, deep blue. The sunlight skipped on the waves.

"Shit." Holt raked his hand through his hair. "Shit."

"Oh, God." Jamie went pale.

Kaitlin drew in a deep breath as she focused on Emily, dear Emily...and peace descended. "She's fine." She had no idea where the words, the certainty had come from. But she knew. Knew there was no reason to worry. Every eye snapped to her.

God, she hated that. When people stared.

"Are you...sure?" Tara asked.

"I'm sure." In fact—

The back door opened and Emily slipped in, making herself small, as though she might go unnoticed.

She did not.

She looked disheveled. Her hair, which was always perfectly coiffed was decidedly...*uncoiffed*. Her makeup was slightly smeared... and her aura was all swirly. Kaitlin tipped her head in an attempt to read the colors.

Something had happened.

Something big.

"Where the hell have you been?" Bella demanded. "I went to your room this morning and your bed hadn't been slept in."

"I told you she was safe," Kaitlin murmured.

"Damn it, Emily," Bella's voice rose into a wail. "We've been worried sick."

Emily nibbled her lip. "I'm sorry. Ash took me out for a ride on his Jet Ski last night—"

"Last night?" Tara chirped. She glanced meaningfully at the clock on the wall.

Bella's nose wrinkled. "Ash?" She shot a look at Holt, who bristled.

"And the motor conked out."

Holt snarled. A little bit. "The...motor conked out?"

"We-we had to spend the night on the island." A blush flooded her cheeks.

All hell broke loose.

Drew wandered in on the scene, and both he and Holt went into Neanderthal mode, bellowing at Emily and barking questions.

Oh dear. Poor Emily. She was nearly as sensitive as Kaitlin. They had no idea what they were doing to her, battering her with these hostile waves. This interrogation—about something so intimate— must be mortifying. Her colors, which had been so clear and sparkling when she'd come in, were now cloudy. Kaitlin set her hand on Emily's back and stroked.

The questioning continued with Drew and Holt and everyone joining in.

Emily's tension rose to an unbearable level as they all peppered questions at her until she finally snapped and ran up the stairs to her room. And slammed the door.

Kaitlin winced. Emily never slammed anything.

"Well you've done it now." Bella glared at Drew, who had done most of the yelling.

"What?" He waved his hand manically. "She went out with some strange guy. Spent the night with some strange guy! Emily!"

Emily. Who had always been as timid with men as Kaitlin. And for good reason.

"You upset her," Kaitlin said softly.

Drew's expression fell. "I'm sorry Kaitlin. I didn't mean to—"

"I'm not the one you need to apologize to."

His shoulders slumped. "Should I go talk to her?"

"No!" A chorus. All the women. In tandem.

"Make her breakfast," Bella said, patting him on the shoulder. "That will make her feel better."

"Breakfast?"

"French toast."

"Pancakes," Jamie countered.

"And don't forget the bacon."

"Do you think she would like that?" Drew asked Kaitlin.

Bella nodded solemnly. "Yeah. She would."

CHAPTER SIX

Jamie and Bella followed Kaitlin up to Emily's room—which was annoying. She needed a friend right now, one who understood better than anyone what had really happened. Not overzealous friends who wanted to barrage her with more questions.

As it was, Bella and Jamie only made things worse. It took a while for Kaitlin to get them to shoo and by the time she did, Emily was crying in earnest.

It broke Kaitlin's heart.

Emily was the gentlest soul she knew. Whatever had happened to her, she needed healing, support. Her colors were tangled in a way Kaitlin couldn't interpret. But there was something different about her. Something had changed.

A vision filled her mind. A cabin. Darkened but by a crackling fire. A man and a woman. Entangled. A—

Good gravy. Kaitlin froze. Heat walked up the back of her neck. Emily...and Ash.

And yes, it was as Kaitlin had suspected. Emily had, indeed, spent the night with Ash Bristol. Given herself to him.

For someone like Emily, who had been as scarred as Kaitlin by an incident long in the past—someone who had deliberately and determinedly avoided men—this was monumental.

She folded her friend into a hug. "Oh, Em. Are you going to be okay?" she murmured into her hair.

"I think so." But she wasn't. Her aura took on a murky gray hue. "I'm not sure what happens now. I kind of got the sense he was withdrawing. You know, when we came back. He didn't want to talk about it or hang out together or anything."

A skirl of trepidation washed through Kaitlin. If Ash had used Emily, just for a one night stand, it would devastate her. Especially after everything she'd been through. "Men can be that way," she said calmingly, as though she knew. "Do you really like him?"

"Yes."

"Then we need to talk to him. To see where he stands." It would be better for Emily if she knew, for certain, where Ash stood. Otherwise she would make herself sick fretting over it. "Do you want to go for a walk?"

"Now?"

Kaitlin nodded. "Now." There was no sense in letting her worry fester.

When they came downstairs, the others lunged forward—perhaps to pepper Emily again. Kaitlin shot them all a warning look. She wrapped her arm around Emily's waist and led her out the door.

No one followed.

Thank God for small favors.

They said nothing on the short walk to Ash's house. What was there to say? Kaitlin focused on calming Emily, sending her healing energy, urging her to be brave. This was one of the defining moments in her life—and there weren't many. How she handled this could change the course of her life journey.

Kaitlin's steps faltered when she saw Ash lounging in a lawn chair by his dock drinking beer. It was early. Far too early for drinking. And then her breath caught when she saw who he was with.

Oh, Parker, certainly—a trill of excitement at that—and Devlin...but Richie too.

Richie ogled her as they approached. Sent her a snarky smirk. Her fingers curled into fists.

Devlin said something and Parker's head snapped up. He stared at her with eyes wide. She shook her head, an unspoken warning, and glanced at Ash.

Emily lifted a hand. "Hey Ash."

"Her?" Richie hissed. "Is she the one?"

Kaitlin winced as she felt pain spearing Emily. She felt it, tasted the chagrin that he had told his friends about their night together. Kaitlin shot Ash a glower. How dare he? *How dare he?* She nodded to Emily, encouraging her to be bold. To ask what needed to be asked.

"Ash, could we...talk?"

"Sure. What do you want to talk about?" He set down his beer and stood.

"I think you know."

"Over here?" To his credit, Ash guided Emily away from his leering friends, where they could speak privately.

Kaitlin tried to focus on Emily, to keep her surrounded by a protective light. At the same time, dueling energies battered her. Something gentle and sweet from Parker—which she really wanted to focus on. And something nasty and bitter from Richie.

He was thinking about fucking her.

Her blood pressure rose.

Thinking about tossing her on the ground and forcing his cock into her—God.

Heat scorched her, and not a pleasant kind.

She whirled on him and sent him a blistering glare.

He smirked.

She allowed her rage to rise—which she rarely did. Her gift was not to be used for revenge or power, but she couldn't help herself. His thoughts were filthy and violent and disturbing. She never wanted him to touch her, talk to her or think of her again.

So she did the only thing she knew how to do. The only thing she could do to protect herself from his malevolence.

She went on the attack.

"You should be ashamed of yourself," she snapped.

He threw back his head and laughed. "You liked it," he smirked.

She'd known such an anemic rebuke would wash over him like water off a duck's back, but she'd thought to try reason before she brought out the big guns. This was the way he wanted to play it? Fine. She sucked in a deep breath and searched his soul, dug deeper. Flinched. It was a foul and wretched place, his soul.

"What would your *mother* say if she knew what you did?"

Richie froze. Paled. "Wh-what?"

"Would she be proud of you, Richie?"

"What are you—do you know my...m-mother?"

"Or your sister? What would she say?"

He began to shake. Took a swig of his beer, but kept his eyes locked on her. "Jesus…"

"Do not—ever—touch me again. If you so much as *think* about it, I will take you out. Do you understand?"

"I have no idea what she's talking about. Do you know what she's talking about?" Richie snarled at his friends. Devlin looked away, but Parker leveled Richie with a cold frown.

"I do. I was there last night, remember ass wipe?"

"Last night?" Devlin's head jerked back. "What happened last night?"

Parker glowered. A muscle bunched in his cheek. "And I promise you this, Richie, if you try some shit like that again, *she* won't have to take you out. I will."

"Jesus God." Richie snarled and focused his attention on the trees. "Not this shit again." He turned to complain to Devlin, "He's been on me like a terrier about it."

"About. What?" Devlin's fingers curled into fists.

"I was fucking drunk, okay. Jesus, woman. I'm sorry."

He wasn't sorry. Kaitlin knew it. They all did. Parker bristled, but Kaitlin sent him a speaking glance. She didn't need him to defend her. She might be small, and she might be slightly fey, but she could defend herself. She knew how to wound.

"Drunk or not, if you touch me again, you're going to lose something you value." She stared at him, letting the message sink in. She didn't specify what he might be losing, because it was not necessary. Rather, she let her certitude suffuse her words. Let her psychic power off the leash.

Like a thundercloud, her energy swept toward him, slammed into him, engulfed him. She let her fury out. Let it rain on him.

Shame curled around him, twined with displeasure and mortification. He gasped for breath. His face went white. His beer wobbled.

"Leave me alone," she repeated in a low, hard voice, underscoring the spiritual message she'd sent.

His head bobbed. Lips flapped. She doubted he'd learned his lesson, but she was certain he would avoid her like the plague in future.

Being a little crazy had its advantages.

Shaking with reaction, she whipped around and refocused on

Emily and Ash. And—

Oh dear.

Emily's expression—usually open and bright—was shuttered. Her face was pale and her and her body shook. Her fingers were curled and her spine straight. The colors swirling around her—sorrow, pain, betrayal—were horrifying. She said something to Ash and turned back for the house, without even waiting for Kaitlin.

Oh. Oh dear.

Her gaze shot to Ash. And she knew.

It *had* been a one-night stand. He'd used Emily and tossed her aside.

She had no fury for him, this poor sad creature who had just broken her friend's heart. Because he'd thrown away the best thing that had ever happened to him.

Without a glance at Parker, she followed Emily back to the house. Emily would need her.

Parker had needed her this morning, and she'd given him what he sought. She'd done it with a whole heart and didn't regret it in the slightest.

But deep in her soul, torment reigned. How on earth could she want to *be* with a man who chose friends like this?

Parker watched her go, torn between regret and a swelling pride. It was amazing the way she stood up to Richie, the way she'd taken him down a peg. He'd never seen such brazen courage in such a tiny package. She was like a warrior princess, there with her hands on her hips, her eyes blazing fire. Her hair flowing over her shoulders and teased by the breeze. He hadn't understood her references to his mother and sister, but whatever it had meant, it had hit Richie where he lived. He'd never seen anyone or anything have that effect on the jerk. In fact, he limped around the house for the rest of the weekend like a whipped dog.

Kinda fun to watch.

As satisfying as it had been to watch her *spank* Richie, he wished the turd hadn't been there when she came by. Wished no one had.

He hadn't seen her coming, hadn't realized she was there until Devlin had muttered something about a hot chick. He'd looked up. Seen her. And been pole axed.

Not that she'd been on his mind, filling it with hopes and dreams about what could be with a woman like her…but she had.

He hadn't stopped thinking about her. Her face, her curves, her smile. Her touch.

Something about her *reached* him where it was dark and deep. Something about her lit the shadows.

He longed to see her again.

But he didn't.

Even though he wandered on the beach all afternoon on Saturday and the better part of Sunday, he didn't see her again. Not until he boarded the ferry to go home. She was there, with her friends, in the corner. She was surrounded by them.

Whenever he glanced at her or tried to catch her eye, one of the men in her group would glower at him.

It probably didn't help that he was sitting with Richie and Ash. If they knew what had happened at the bar on Friday night, or what had happened between them on Saturday…he was lucky all they did was glare.

He couldn't take it. Sitting there, not looking at her. Knowing whatever it had been was probably over—especially after what had happened between Ash and her friend. So he went out on the deck and stood at the back of the boat and peered down into the frothing wake and thought about her. The wind was cold for summer. It buffeted him. He didn't care. He jammed his hands into the pockets of his windbreaker.

"Parker."

Her voice was soft, but still, a punch to the gut.

He whirled around. "Kaitlin…"

She smiled. Oh, thank God, she smiled.

He opened his mouth to say something, but couldn't form words. She was so beautiful, her hair a tousled tangle in the wind, her cheeks pink. Her eyes bright. Lovely. An angel.

She leaned on the rail by his side and stared out at where they'd been. "Oh!" she cried, pointing up into the sky.

It was hard, following her gaze. Hard ripping his focus from her face. But he did. An eagle soared overhead, wings wide, calling to the wind.

"Beautiful." A whisper. All he could force out.

"Isn't it?" She sighed. "I love living here."

"I do too. Um, have you always lived here?" Yeah. Small talk. He could probably do small talk. Plus, he really wanted to know. He wanted to know everything about her.

She shook her head. "We lived in Los Angeles when I was a child. Well..." she snorted a laugh. "Not Los Angeles. Encino. Like, the Valley?"

He tried to bite back a smile at her Val Girl accent and then didn't bother. "Did you like living there?"

"I did. The sunshine, the vibe. The bustle of the place. But my mother hated it. So we moved here."

"Is it just you and your mom?"

She nodded. "My aunt joined us when I was twelve." Her smile dimmed. "She just passed away."

"I'm sorry."

"Me too."

"And your dad?"

She didn't answer. Just shook her head. His gaze fixated on her lower lip. The way she nibbled it. He wanted to nibble it. He wanted to kiss her. He wanted—

"There you are!" A booming voice invaded their bubble, bursting it with a jarring tenor. A bulky man—one of her friends, the one who had met her at the door the night Parker had walked her home—pushed between them.

He liked to think the look she shot him was apologetic, that there was a thread of regret in it.

"Drew." She smiled at him.

The big guy shuddered. "It's cold out here. Let's go inside, Kait." He looped his arm around her waist and tried to draw her away.

Everything in Parker rebelled at the thought.

"But it's so beautiful. Look, Drew! See how the sun hits the water there? A rainbow."

"This is the Pacific Northwest," he said on a snort. "There are always rainbows somewhere."

She glared at him. "No there aren't. Let me enjoy this."

He frowned, but went quiet, standing between them like a defender. Or a boyfriend.

But if Drew was her boyfriend, would she have come home with him the other day? Would she have unzipped his jeans? Would she have taken him in her hands? Her mouth?

He studied the guy with an assessing eye.

No. She would not have done all those things.

But it was clear, this Drew character had the hots for her.

"What do you do?" he asked him, just to make conversation, although a part of him really wanted to know. Wanted to gauge the competition. If he was, indeed, someone she *liked*. His gut flipped at the thought.

"Drew's a firefighter," Kaitlin said, when Drew answered only with a frown. She patted the bastard's arm.

"Really?" Parker had a special place in his heart for firefighters. One of them had saved his life. "That must be interesting."

"Totally," Drew drawled. "And what do you do...?"

"Parker." This from Kaitlin, who seemed to know Drew was fishing for his name. He wouldn't have given it. Two could play at this game.

"I'm a lawyer."

Drew's features bunched up. Yeah. Probably not what he wanted to hear. He'd probably been hoping for *grocery bagger* or *arsonist*.

"You're a lawyer?" Again, Kaitlin. Her eyes lit up. Hell, her whole face lit up. "What kind of law do you practice?"

"I'm a divorce attorney."

Fuck. He hated the way her sweet expression soured. "That's...nice." She turned back to stare at the sea, threading her fingers together.

"Make a lot of money at that?" Drew's tone was contemptuous. Why? Parker had no clue. People getting divorces needed attorneys too.

"I do okay." Silence settled around them, but for the whip of the wind in his ears. It was uncomfortable. Parker searched for something to say. "What do you do, Kaitlin?" he asked, though Drew bristled when he said her name. As though he was the only man who had the right.

She glanced at Drew before she answered. Nibbled her lip again. "I, ah, I'm kind of a therapist."

Drew snorted a laugh.

Kaitlin shot him a frown.

"What kind of therapist?"

Did he imagine the flush rising on her face? "I, ah, help people who are in pain."

How like her. She'd helped him. Did she have any idea how much she helped him? "A physical therapist then."

Her lashes fluttered. "Something like that. Yes. Oh, look." She pointed to the sky again. "Now there are two of them." And indeed, two eagles wheeled through the sky, catching the wind and soaring higher, flirting with each other. "I wonder if one of them is the one we saved?"

Her eyes were bright. She seemed so hopeful. He didn't have the heart to mention there were thousands of eagles in these islands. "Probably."

Yeah. The lie was worth her smile.

"You saved an eagle?" This, apparently, pissed Drew off. "When?"

"On Saturday. I went for a walk in the morning and we saw it there, trapped in a tree. Parker cut it loose." She gazed at him as though he'd hung the moon.

Drew didn't. If looks could kill, Parker would be six feet under. In fact, he wouldn't put it past Drew to tip him over the rail into the propellers.

"*We?*" he clipped. "Kaitlin, you really shouldn't go walking in the morning."

She gaped at Drew. "What? Are you serious?"

"The tide. A tsunami. A tree could fall."

Her laughter was a melody. "Drew, you are so silly." She tipped her head back up to the eagles and sighed. While her attention was so engaged, Drew took the opportunity to glower at Parker. His meaning was plain. *Get lost.*

Parker grinned and rocked back on his heels. Yeah, he wasn't going anywhere.

Drew narrowed his eyes. And then he said, "You know, when eagles mate they often die?"

Kaitlin gasped.

Yeah, Drew had won her attention again, but at what cost? She was horrified. "No."

"Yeah," he continued gleefully. "They fly way high and mate up there." He waved at the sky. "Since they're joined, they can't fly and they plummet to the earth in a death spiral. If they don't disengage before they hit the ground, they die."

God. He looked so pleased with himself. Parker wanted to punch him. And not just so he would stop looking so smug. But because he'd brought tears to Kaitlin's beautiful eyes.

"Drew, that's terrible. Why would you say that?"

His brow rumpled. "Because it's true." He glanced from Kaitlin to Parker. "It is. Google it."

"I'm not going to Google it." She spun away, storming to a spot a few feet away. Parker followed. Drew did not.

Like a reprimanded child, he tromped back inside. But the glower he sent Parker wasn't childlike at all.

Kaitlin blew out a breath and Parker settled at her side. She seemed to scoot closer. "Are you cold?" he asked.

"A little. But this is too lovely to go inside."

It was. Lovely.

He curled his arm around her shoulder and pulled her closer. She smiled at him. His heart fluttered.

That had never happened before.

His heart had never fluttered.

It was disconcerting. Maybe he should ask Doctor Marks about that on Monday.

As though she could read his mind, she asked, "How is your cut?"

"It's fine." It was. It would be. He wasn't thinking about it now. He was thinking about her. This woman. In his arms. "Kaitlin…"

"Yes?"

Words failed him. The look on her face, so open, so welcoming, nearly brought him to his knees. "I'd like to…see you again."

She blossomed. Her smile swelled. Her eyes shone. Her lips parted. "I'd like that very much."

"Dinner some night this week?" And then he remembered. He had a big case to work on. One that could make or break his career with Barstow and Rank. At this stage in the game, there were always late nights, hurried meetings and panicked texts.

But hell. He wanted to see her again.

Maybe just one evening. The case could wait. Couldn't it?

"I'm free on Thursday." Her smile was a little shy. Very sweet.

He leaned closer. "Thursday would be perfect. What do you like to eat?"

She sighed. "Anything."

"How about Tom's Surf and Turf. It's near Montlake on Lake Washington."

Her eyes lit up. "I love that place. Okay. What time should we meet?"

Meet? His belly dipped. She didn't want him to pick her up. But yeah…it was probably too early to be exchanging addresses. He forced a smile. "How about six?"

"Six would be wonderful."

"Perfect." Exhilaration whipped through him…until he turned. His attention stalled on three burly men standing at the window, glaring out at the deck. Drew, of course, and two of his friends. Holt Lamm and Cam Jackson, if he wasn't mistaken. They all had identical expressions. Furious expressions.

Parker shot them a grin and then turned back to Kaitlin. He tipped his head toward the battalion. "But if you could? Leave your guard dogs at home?"

She glanced over her shoulder and then threw her head back with a laugh.

And he laughed too as elation trilled through him.

Because he was going to see her again in four days.

And then despair.

How the hell was he going to make it that long?

But he didn't see her.

He missed their rendezvous. It devastated him, but he missed it.

To his surprise, it wasn't work that scuttled his plans. It was family.

Which was odd, because Parker had no family. They had all perished in the fire that had nearly claimed his life.

On Wednesday, his world imploded. Ash called to say that his father had had a massive heart attack and was on his deathbed. Something cold invaded Parker's soul at the news. Adam Bristol was as close to a father as he'd ever had. And Ash was like a brother. He couldn't not respond to the call. He couldn't not go sit with his friend as they waited for news.

In retrospect, he realized he should have asked for her number. For something.

But, giddy with excitement, it had slipped his mind.

So he missed their date.

It just about killed him.

CHAPTER SEVEN

Kaitlin was floating on a cloud when she returned home from the island. Her mind was filled with thoughts of Parker—and her heart as well. There was something about him, something magical perhaps.

When he'd slipped his arm around her on the deck of the ferry, she'd felt protected and warm. And there had been no pain, no snarl of sensation whatsoever. It was peaceful being with him, despite the angst and dark memories that sometimes surrounded him.

She could tell her presence was a balm to him as well.

She was a healer. It was part of her job. But her gift had never pleased her as much as it did with Parker. They soothed each other, somehow.

The guys were annoyed with her, of course, when she came back inside and took her seat. She could tell from their roiling intent, they wanted to pepper her with questions, the way they'd peppered Emily, but Kaitlin did not allow it.

When Cam sat back and crossed his arms and drawled, "So…" she'd shot him a cool glance and his lips had snapped shut and that had been the end of it.

Drew was another story altogether.

He'd always been a hoverer, but now it seemed he was a hoverer on steroids. He called her that night as she made herself a bowl of soup for dinner. He wanted to come over. She told him no.

He called her at work and texted her several times the next day and then the next. After a while, she quit taking his calls. To which he responded by texting more often.

Thursday was her day at the shelter. She was in a session with Susan and Lily when her phone buzzed, once again. She didn't need to check it to know it was Drew.

She loved him, really she did, but if he didn't back off, she was going to have to smack him. It was an annoying intrusion because she was nervous about her date with Parker. If she weren't humming with excitement and trepidation, she wouldn't have minded. But as it was, each buzz from her phone set her teeth on edge.

"Do you need to take that?" Susan asked.

Kaitlin set it to 'silence' and dropped it into her purse. She hated that he was interrupting her work. "No." She smiled and patted Susan's hand. While the sweet woman was getting better, there were still some nasty bruises on her cheek. She tried to cover them up with makeup, but some bruises refused to be hidden. "So tell me," Kaitlin said, forcing her attention back where it belonged…on her clients. "How is Lily doing?"

Susan sighed and gazed at her daughter who was playing with dolls in the corner. Dolls were helpful, Kaitlin found, in working through the pain. Lily held the boy doll up in front of the girl doll and then bashed them together making *'Kussssh Kusssssh'* sounds. "She's…okay."

"It will take some time." Kaitlin nibbled on her lip. Possibly the memory would never be wiped away. "Any word?"

Susan flinched.

Kaitlin felt a thread of remorse for the question, but she needed to know.

"He wants custody."

Kaitlin froze. She glanced at Lily, the adorable three year old, whose father had sent her to the hospital with a broken arm. Her cast was a brash reminder of his fury.

Susan shook her head. "He doesn't want custody. He wants power. Over me. But I can't let him have her. I can't." Panic rose in her voice.

"You're safe here." Kaitlin sent her a calming wave. "No one knows you're here."

"But what if—"

"He won't find you." She forced a smile. "That's what we do here. We keep women safe."

"He has money. He has friends. He could track us…"

"Then we'll move you. Susan. Look at me." Kaitlin touched her face, to the side, where the swelling wasn't so bad. "You're safe here. You need to focus on getting better. Let me help."

"I...okay."

Kaitlin stood and walked behind her and placed her hands on Susan's slender shoulders and began to work.

She forced all thoughts of Drew and Parker and everyone else from her mind and focused on this. On what mattered. On helping someone heal.

The pain was excruciating.

When she went home that night, she ate an entire chocolate bar. One of the big ones.

Drew called just as she was getting ready for her date with Parker. If she hadn't been so frazzled—changing outfits six times—she wouldn't have picked up.

"Hey, babe." His warm voice flooded over the line. "What are you doing?"

"Oh. Hi, Drew. I'm kind of busy."

"Yeah. Okay. So I was thinking about going to the island this weekend. Are you going to be there?"

She juggled the phone as she tossed another dress onto the bed. Maybe this one was better? "I can't this weekend Drew. I'm helping Emily prepare for a charity thing."

"Ug," he snorted. "She roped you in?"

These shoes? Or these? Kaitlin laid them out on the bed side by side and studied them. She tried to tap into Parker's energy, to assess which he would prefer, but Drew kept chattering in her ear.

"She's a storm trooper when it comes to those charity things. Which one is this?"

"Teen Waystation."

"Oh yeah. I think she mentioned that this weekend."

"It's important to her." Okay. The black ones. Not too high of a heel, but not too casual.

"So...what are you doing for dinner tonight?"

"I have a date." She winced as soon as the words left her lips. *Good gravy.* She could feel his hurt wafting toward her over the line.

Silence. And then, "A...date?"

Kaitlin sighed. "Yes, Drew. A date."

"With *him*?"

Really, it was none of his business. Except he was her friend. And he cared. And he deserved better than to be sloughed off or lied to. "I really like him, Drew."

"He's a jerk!"

"He's not."

"Kaitlin, don't go."

She took a deep cleansing breath and sent him a calming wave too. It didn't work. The threads connecting them bristled with tension. "Drew, I really like him. He's...different."

"Everybody's *different*."

"Not like Parker."

Drew made a sound, something like a snarl. "I'm coming over."

"No, Drew, don't—"

But he'd disconnected.

Kaitlin glanced at the clock and figured she had about ten minutes to get dressed and get out of the house before Drew showed up. It was probably cowardly to run like this, run and hide, but she really didn't have the inclination to fight with him about this.

She grabbed the dress on the top of the pile and the shoes closest at hand and got dressed. Ripping a brush through her hair and grabbing her purse, she bolted.

Needless to say, she was early for their date. She got a table and ordered a sparkling water and waited for Parker. And waited. And waited. All the while, trying to ignore her panic as the minutes ticked by. The time for their date came and went.

After an hour, she ordered her dinner, to go, and took it home in a humiliating white box.

She tried to disregard the devastation welling within her.

He'd stood her up.

Worse than that, she didn't have his number, or anything. She had no way to contact him again.

As wonderful as it had been, as wonderful as *he* had been, it was over.

She snorted a laugh to herself as she got out of her car and headed for her little house on Queen Anne Hill overlooking the Seattle skyline. Yeah. She hadn't seen that coming.

Wasn't that the way it always was? Infinite universal truths exposed to her—in the shower—but something that really mattered to her? A mystery.

Thank God she had chocolate in the cupboard. She was going to need it tonight.

But ah. As if being stood up by Parker weren't bad enough, Drew was lounging on her stoop. It was embarrassing to have to explain her tears to him. Painful beyond bearing to have him wrap her in his arms and hold her while she told her tale of woe.

Crushing to have to stop him when he tried to kiss her later, and see his wounded expression.

It broke her heart.

He loved her. *Loved her.*

He was a wonderful person and a marvelous friend, if a little too persistent.

Why couldn't she just love Drew?

Why did life have to be so difficult?

Parker sat in the uncomfortable plastic chair in the hospital cafeteria and stared at his hands. His fingers were linked so tightly, his knuckles were white.

It had been a hell of a week. Thank God it was Friday, though the weekend wasn't looking any better. On top of the devastation of Adam being so sick, he'd missed his date with Kaitlin yesterday when his mentor had had another heart attack.

He would probably never see her again.

To make matters even worse, work sucked balls. The case he was embroiled in was slippery, a nasty divorce, and the client was an important one.

Barstow had poked his head into Parker's office on Monday and smiled. That in itself was horrifying. But then his boss had gone on to say, *"We're counting on you Rieth. Counting on you to make this happen. If you can pull this off and please Tucker, that corner office is yours."*

Just like that. The office was his.

All he had to do was pull some freaking rabbit out of a hat.

Hell, he couldn't even serve the papers.

Tucker's wife had run off to the south of France or someplace like that. How did you serve papers on someone you couldn't find?

Parker had Gilley on it. Gilley was one of the best P.I.s on the payroll. If anyone could find Mrs. Tucker, it would be him. But it had been over a week with absolutely no news. No records of transit, no hits on her passport and nothing on her credit cards.

He didn't know why it was suddenly *his* responsibility to find Susan Tucker, but it was.

He sighed and scrubbed his neck, though it didn't ease the pinging of his migraine. The headaches had come back in the last day or so. There had been a glorious release from them, but only for a short time. He tracked the reprieve to the moment he'd seen Kaitlin. Touched her. Possibly when she'd taken him in her mouth.

But he couldn't think about that. About her. Not here. Not now.

He hated hospitals. Always had. The smell, the squeak of the nurses' shoes, the *whispers*. Even the fluorescent lights gave him the heebie jeebies. He glared up at them.

He should just go home. Ash had, for God's sake. Ash and Michelle and Trish...they'd all gone. Adam's surgery was tomorrow and they wanted to be fresh. Besides, Ash had said, there was nothing more they could do here tonight.

But Parker didn't see it that way. Staying here, standing vigil, felt like something.

Too bad the food sucked. He poked at his cherry pie. It bled. Some neon red, cherry-like substance. He didn't know why he'd gotten it. Probably just to have something to poke.

He tried to pretend it wasn't Drew.

He tried not to think of *her*.

A laugh at the register caught his attention. His heart jolted. His breath snagged. His head whipped up and, *holy shit*, there she was.

He didn't bother to wonder why she was here at the hospital. Or so late at night. Or if he was, perhaps, hallucinating. When she picked up a cardboard container and nodded at the cashier and headed for the door he leapt to his feet and called her name.

Tried to call her name. It clogged in his throat.

Panicked, he ran after her—although it felt like slow motion.

Oh hell.

How horrible would it be to lose her now? When he'd found her again?

He rounded the corner to see her step on the elevator. She turned and pressed the button and the doors slid closed.

Desolation slithered through him.

And then, their eyes met. Hers widened in surprise through the ever shrinking crack.

In a moment. In a moment, she would be gone.

But no. She thrust her hand between the doors and stopped them. She stepped out, toward him, her lips parted, her features rumpled.

"Parker?" Her voice was like a balm. It shivered over his skin. He shuddered.

"Kaitlin." Thank God. He'd caught her.

She glanced around the empty hallway. "What are you doing here?"

"I, ah..." He poked his finger toward the ceiling. "Someone's in the hospital."

"I'm sorry." She touched his hand. A skim, nothing more. His headache abated. Or he was delusional. "That's terrible."

Yeah. It was.

"They won't let me see him." He didn't know why he said that. Of course they wouldn't let him in to see Adam. Only family was allowed in and...he wasn't family. He felt like family, though. Fury at the stupid hospital rules swelled up in him. He tried to swallow it down.

"Do you...want to talk?"

God. She always just seemed to know what he needed.

"Do you have time?"

She smiled. "Of course. I'm off duty now."

Together, they walked back to the plastic cafeteria and sat at his table with the bleeding pie and ice cold coffee. Her attention fell on his plate and her nose curled up.

"You shouldn't have gotten the cherry pie," she said.

"Tell me about it."

"The chocolate cream is pretty good."

"Maybe I should get some of that." He was not inclined to move. Couldn't bear to walk away from her. Even for pie.

She tipped her head and curled her hair behind her ear. "Do you want me to get some for you?"

"No. I don't really want pie." He poked the slice again, just to make a point. "I'm sorry I missed our date. I was here. And I didn't have your number."

"It's okay." But he noticed she lowered her lashes. He hadn't known her long, but he could tell when she told a lie. She always dropped her gaze when she lied.

"Did-did you wait long?"

"No." Another lie.

Shit. He raked his fingers through his hair. "I was really looking forward to it."

"So was I." Thank God, she met his gaze at that.

"Maybe we should try again?"

She tipped her chin. Toyed with a fork.

Silence stretched between them, punctuated by the beat of his heart. Finally she said, "So who's your friend?"

"My...what?"

"Your friend. In the hospital."

"My... um, Ash's dad. He had a heart attack."

"Ah. So he's up on four."

Parker nodded. He'd spent a lot of time on four lately.

"I'm so sorry. Are you close?"

Parker snorted. He didn't mean to snort. It was terribly disrespectful. He hoped she understood. "He was...is like a father to me."

"I see." And she did, didn't she? She seemed to understand everything.

"I'm worried that—"

She covered his hand. "That you won't get to see him again?"

"He's having surgery tomorrow. Open heart." He forced back some cold coffee. It was hideous.

"It's a shame you can't see him."

"Yeah. It's killing me."

She sat back and studied him. While it hurt when she drew away, her gaze was warm, comforting. Then, unaccountably, she grinned. It was a wicked grin. "Come with me," she said, grabbing hold of his sleeve.

"Where."

"We're going to four."

He followed her, although he didn't know why, other than the bald fact that he would probably follow her anywhere she led. When they stepped into the elevator, she threaded her fingers in his. Her smile broadened. She raised up on her toes in a little bounce.

Damn. Everything about her was joyful.

Everything.

The door dinged open and she sailed out as though she owned the place, still clutching his hand. She smiled at the grumpy nurse guarding the ICU wing. "Hey Clara," she chirped.

Clara—and apparently that was her name, not Battleaxe as he had assumed—smiled back. Astonishing, considering…what a battleaxe she was. "Well, hello there Kaitlin. We haven't seen you in a while. How have you been, honey?"

"I'm good. Real good. I, ah… could we see Adam Bristol?"

"Adam Bristol?" Clara's caterpillar brows rose. She glanced at Parker and her familiar sour mien slipped into place.

"Just for a minute. Please?"

Clara shuffled some papers and grumbled a little bit, but in the end, she relented. "All right," she said, handing them facemasks. "But just for a minute. He's got surgery in the morning. He's in four-oh-six."

And as easily as that, he was in. Through those heavy double doors marked *CARDIAC UNIT: ABSOLUTELY NO ADMITTANCE* and on his way down the echoey hall toward Adam's room.

Still, she held his hand.

She was a miracle, his Kaitlin. A miracle.

The look she sent him as she gave him the mask, and showed him how to sanitize his hands, was scintillating. Playful and hopeful and sweet.

He probably shouldn't have thought about kissing her when she put her finger to her lips to remind him to be quiet. But he did.

She pushed open the door and led him into a shadowed room. The sounds of machines and monitors intruded on the hush. Parker stopped, stock-still at the sight of Adam Bristol on the bed. He was washed in a halo of light from the dim lamp heading the bed. He seemed so frail, so diminished—that strong impervious man who had been the sole pillar in his life—Parker wanted to turn around and run.

But Kaitlin didn't allow it. She tugged him closer. "Mr. Bristol," she said softly. And then, when he didn't respond, she laid her hand on his. "Mr. Bristol, there's someone here to see you."

Adam's lashes fluttered, opened. His eyes were watery and streaked with red. His lips, pale and cracked.

But they curved upward when Adam saw him. "Parker," he croaked. "Parker, my boy." He lifted his arm, despite all the tubes, and reached out. Parker rushed to his side, and grabbed it.

"Dad." He didn't intend for that word to come out. But Adam didn't seem to mind. He tightened his hold in an anemic squeeze.

"Well, I must be doing better if they let you in."

"Of course. Of course you're doing better."

"Got some damn surgery tomorrow." So like Adam. So gruff in the face of dread.

"You're going to come through it just fine. Just fine."

"Did you see Michelle?"

"Yeah. We had dinner."

Adam snorted. "Here?"

"Mmm hmm." Parker had to chuckle at Adam's grimace. "I know. Not the Ritz. But just think, before you know it, you'll be home eating a thick steak and Trish's glazed carrots."

Another grimace. Trish's glazed carrots were legendary. For being hideous. Ash's sister was not what one would call a gourmet cook. Or...a cook at all.

Adam's gaze swung to Kaitlin. "And who is this pretty thing?"

Parker pulled her forward. "Kaitlin, meet Adam Bristol. Adam, this is Kaitlin."

"You are a pretty thing. Single?" Adam's brow arched.

Kaitlin nodded.

"Hmm. I have a son about your age, you know."

Parker frowned and Adam laughed.

"Yes, I've met your son, Mr. Bristol," she said, once again setting her hand on his. It lingered there. "He's very...nice." She glanced away.

Yeah. A lie. After the way Ash had dumped her friend, her opinion of him was likely in the toilet. But Parker appreciated that she was gracious and gentle with Adam.

"So, you're having a little surgery tomorrow?" she asked, running her palm over Adam's chest. She was so matter of fact about it, it didn't even strike Parker as odd...until later. Her hand stilled over his heart and she closed her eyes, breathed in deep and then exhaled in a soft gush. "Mmm. Yes. You have a strong heart, Mr. Bristol."

"Why thank you, young lady." It was probably Parker's imagination, or the proximity of a 'pretty thing,' but Adam's color looked better. His grin widened.

She patted him softly. "I think you're going to come through this just fine."

Clara barged in, just then, to smile at Kaitlin and frown at Parker, which somehow she managed to do at the same time. "Ahem," she said, as though that said everything. Then again, it did.

"We have to go now, Mr. Bristol," Kaitlin said softly. "I'll try to come back and see you after the surgery." She waggled a finger at him. "You be good now."

"I will." He winked. "I will."

As they left, Kaitlin took Parker's hand again. "What do you say about trying that chocolate pie now?" she asked.

"Okay." Hell yeah. Anything to extend this chance meeting. This time he would *not* fail to get her phone number. "So… Do you really think he'll be okay?" he asked as they stepped onto the elevator.

Her smile was beatific. "Yes," she said. "He'll be just fine."

And Parker believed her.

For one thing, he couldn't bear the alternative.

And for another…she seemed to know what she was talking about.

He asked her out over chocolate pie—and damn, could that girl put away the chocolate pie. To his delight they made plans to have dinner the next night, if, of course, Adam did well in his surgery, which she seemed to think he would. She gave him her phone number—he memorized it immediately—as well as her address.

And somehow, all of a sudden, all was well with the world.

CHAPTER EIGHT

Kaitlin was nervous as all get out as she prepared for her date with Parker.

She couldn't deny the niggle of dread that he might not show up. Though she understood why he'd missed their previous date, and for good reason, the remnants of her desolation still clung.

It was only dinner. There was no need for such angst, but she couldn't stop herself.

It was a little scary, her feelings for him. How vulnerable he made her feel. And none of her usual tools for psychic self-protection worked. At least, not very well.

She suspected it was because, deep down, she didn't want distance from him.

She didn't want distance at all.

Parker rang the bell at six on the dot—Kaitlin suspected he'd been waiting in his car checking his watch. But then, she'd been hovering in the foyer. She didn't whip the door open before the chime wafted away, but just barely.

He greeted her with a wide smile. A smile that made her heart flutter.

"Kaitlin." He looked magnificent in slacks and a sport coat and a crisply-pressed linen shirt. His tie was sedate, classic, clearly one he wore to work. He held a small box in his hands.

"Parker."

"I, ah…" He nodded to the stained glass window in her front door—a confection of drooping purple wisteria. "I like your window."

"Thank you."

"Your house is nice."

"Thank you. It was my aunt's. She left it to me when she passed. It's over a hundred years old." It had been renovated many times and had all kinds of charming, quirky features. Like the window, and the little room beneath the stairs and—

"It's nice."

"Thank you."

They stared at each other, wrapped in a sudden uneasy cloud.

She hadn't dated much. Didn't know what to do next. And it appeared he didn't either. But then he thrust the box at her. "These are for you."

"Thank you." She realized she sounded a little bit like a very redundant parrot, but she couldn't find the wherewithal to be witty. "What is it?"

"Chocolates." He named a local brand, one she loved, and her apprehension evaporated. Her smile blossomed. And his gaze stalled on her face.

"I love these. Thank you. Um, would you like to come in?"

He paled and shook his head; shyness welled and swelled around him, tinting his aura a light rose. "I, ah, better not." She had the sense he was trying to be chivalrous at all costs, which was adorable. He shifted his feet. "Are you ready to go?"

"Sure." Biting back a grin, she set the chocolates on the table in the hall, collected her coat and followed him to his car. She had no idea why his nervousness somehow made her feel more confident.

They were both wary about this new phase in their relationship. They both wanted things to work out—but weren't sure how to proceed. Perhaps the best approach was just to follow his lead.

He took her to Tom's Surf and Turf—to make up for their missed date. He had reserved a table on the deck overlooking the water and the sparkling lights of Bellevue across the lake. He had fillet mignon and she had scallops. And they talked. They talked for hours. She told him about her life—well, most of it. She did hold some secrets close to her heart. Some things were too intimate for a first date, after all. He told her about his life. Told her he'd been orphaned at five and entered the foster system, which he'd hated. His life changed when Adam Bristol signed up to be his mentor.

She heard a lot about Adam and Ash on that date. Seeing his friend through Parker's eyes, she couldn't help but like him, which made her sad. Emily and Ash would have been so good for each other. They had so much in common and their energies were perfectly matched.

When Parker took her home, he kissed her, a soft buss, on her forehead, and asked her out again.

For the next week or so they went on casual dates. Dinner. A movie. An art showing at Jamie's gallery. The symphony to see her friend Cassie, a famous cellist, play.

And at the end of each date, he took her home and kissed her chastely on the forehead.

While Kaitlin wanted more, and she could tell Parker did too, she sensed he wasn't ready. So she didn't press for more. This was a time of discovery for them. For alignment. And with each interaction, she felt herself moving closer to him. And he to her.

He had to work the night of Emily's charity fund raiser, which was a pity. Kaitlin would have loved for him to attend. He would have enjoyed it.

Ash Bristol showed up unexpectedly, practically on his knees. He'd had a change of heart and Kaitlin had the pleasure of watching him beg Emily for another chance. Emily didn't make him suffer for too long. And why would she? She was besotted with him. The two had always been a good match, but now that his energy had shifted, softened, they fit even more perfectly. Kaitlin hoped, sincerely hoped, there was a chance for them.

After Emily and Ash reunited, and Ash discovered Kaitlin and Parker were dating as well, he suggested they double date and between them, the guys planned a day trip out in the Sound. Fishing.

When they suggested it, she and Emily exchanged wry glances. Fishing had never been Kaitlin's favorite thing, but she loved the idea of spending the whole day with Parker. And Emily loved the water.

Though in the end, it could hardly be called a double date, because Holt came too. Probably to keep an eye on Ash. He was still annoyed about that kerfuffle with Emily, though she'd gotten over it.

And it was hardly a date because the guys pretty much talked fishing—amongst themselves—while Emily and Kaitlin dangled their legs over the side and chatted, or stood on the deck and pretended to fish.

But it was a beautiful day. Clouds flecked the blue sky and the sun shone brightly. The boat bobbed on the water. Waves slapped at the hull as they drifted with their lines in the water.

And Emily and Parker and Holt were here—three of her favorite people.

Even Ash was growing on her.

Ash and Holt had stripped down and were fishing shirtless, their tanned chests soaking in the sunlight, but Parker kept his long-sleeved shirt on. He always wore it. Kaitlin thought of it as his shield.

It was delightful standing on the deck, holding her rod, buffeted by the breeze and the sway of the small craft. Her spirit soared as she stared out at the sparkling sea, listening to the chattered conversations of her dear friends. The guys talked about sports and cars and motorcycles mostly, and when they got hungry, Emily would bring them drinks or sandwiches—she wasn't much of a fisherman either, but she did love being on the water...and she loved being with Ash. It was evident in the glow of happiness around her.

It was all very peaceful. Especially because no one was catching anything.

Probably because, unbeknownst to them, Kaitlin was sending little psychic warnings to the fish.

Poor fishies. They only wanted a snack. It was horrible to think they would bite on what they thought was a perfectly innocent worm—a drowning worm—to have a nasty hook spear into them and yank them from the only home they'd ever—

A warm presence sidled up next to her. She put her hand on her floppy hat, tipped up her face and smiled at him. *Parker.* Warmth suffused her as he stepped close. His aftershave—and the smell of bait and diesel—wafted toward her. She focused on the aftershave.

He tossed out his line and then watched as she reeled in her line and tossed it back out. Then he snorted a laugh. "You realize you're not going to catch anything if you don't use any bait, right?" Humor laced his tone. She loved the way his eyes danced.

She shot him a grin. "Maybe I don't want to catch anything."

"That is kind of the point of fishing." He winked at her.

"I know." She blew out a sigh. "But it makes me sad."

"Sad?" His expression crumpled into a frown.

"Watching them squirm."

He paled and scrubbed his face. "Great. Now if I catch anything,

I'm going to have to set it free. What will we eat for dinner?"

"Pizza?"

His laugh skipped on the breeze. "No anchovies?"

She wrinkled her nose. "Gross."

"Yeah. I thought not." His attention snapped to his pole as the tip bobbed. But then it stopped and he let out a breath. A comfortable silence surrounded them. They stood, side by side, holding their rods and watching the little flecks of white on the waves as the wind kicked up. Her hair danced in the breeze until he tucked it behind her ear. "We could always go to the fish market after," he said.

She made a face. "The one at Pike Place Market?"

"Sure. Why not?"

"They *throw* them at you there."

"Again, also the point."

"Have you ever been hit by a thirty pound salmon?"

"I wouldn't mind." He jiggled his pole and whistled into the wind. "I wouldn't mind catching one either."

But the next time he dropped his line in the water, there was no bait on his hook either.

After the excursion ended—dismally for the men, to Kaitlin's amusement—they all went out to dinner at a wonderful restaurant that brought steamed clams and mussels and King crab legs in a bucket and dumped them on the table. It was noisy and messy and raucous and fun and Kaitlin had a wonderful time.

She loved watching Emily blossom with Ash.

And she loved sitting next to Parker. Because every once in a while, he would touch her knee with his, let his thigh relax against hers on the bench. His warmth soaked into her, excited her.

Their gazes tangled as they both reached for the same crab leg. He smiled and heat sizzled through her.

Because she knew. In that moment, she could tell. He was ready.

Parker's nerves were raw by the time he drove Kaitlin home after their fishing date. He hadn't dated much—especially after that appalling experience with Chandra, who had stared at him in horror when the shirt came off—so he didn't know how to proceed. How many dates were enough before a man asked a woman to share his bed?

But he wanted, he really needed, more from Kaitlin. For one thing, he wanted *her*. She was the most physically attractive woman he'd ever met. But it was more than that. He *liked* her. A lot. Maybe more. The past few weeks had been a mix of heaven and hell. Heaven, because he got to see her so often, and hell…because he got to see her so often.

After each date he kissed her on the forehead and went home hard. The memory of that morning, there in Ash's basement, her mouth around him, haunted him. Fantasies of taking her, loving her, tormented him. He wished he could just slough off his self-consciousness and claim her the way a man—a man who was not wounded and scarred—claims a woman. He wished he could just step into the skin of someone else, if only for a night.

But his fear stopped him.

She hadn't recoiled in disgust when she'd seen his bare chest. It was possible such a thing didn't matter to her. But his logical mind rejected the notion.

What woman would want *him?*

But with each date they grew closer. With each date his courage grew.

He loved how he felt when he was around her. Loved the way he felt about himself when he was with her. As though he was a different kind of man. A man who could be someone's hero, not just an ugly, scarred thing to be pitied.

There was never pity in Kaitlin's eyes.

She accepted him as he was. Scars and all.

He hoped.

Tonight he was going to kiss her. Not on the forehead, but a real kiss. He was going to kiss her and see where it went.

He dared not hope.

But he dared.

He walked her to her porch, as he always did, with his hand on her elbow. But when they stopped at the door and she tipped up her chin, looking at him expectantly, he didn't kiss her forehead. He set his palms on her cheeks and gently angled her face up.

It was just a kiss, he reminded himself. It could become more, but in the beginning, it was just a kiss. Nothing to be nervous about.

His mouth touched hers and she sighed, leaned into him. Excitement scored him. He wrapped his arms around her and pulled her closer and she followed his lead.

He tipped his head to the side to cover her more fully and her lips parted. Her tongue peeped out.

There had been lust, these past few weeks, but nothing like this lust. It rose within him and roared, like a savage beast. His cock surged. His pulse pounded. The urge to shove her back against the wall, rub against her, snarled in his belly. It horrified him.

A woman like Kaitlin deserved gentility. A tender touch. Not a man so stretched on the rack of desire that he would dry hump her on her porch after a date.

He pulled away, released her. Sucked in a breath. Raked his fingers through his hair. "Kaitlin…"

She smiled. A beatific smile. It sent shudders of remorse through him.

How could he? How could he have such base urges for an angel like—

"Would you like to come inside?" Her voice was soft and danced away on the cool night breeze, but he heard it. Hell yeah, he heard it. Every cell in his body hummed.

"Y-yes."

She unlocked the door and took his hand, pulling him inside. He stared at her foyer, as though he'd never seen a foyer before. It was done in art deco. A runner led down the hall to the kitchen. A staircase curved upstairs—

But he didn't let himself think about upstairs.

She'd invited him inside. Maybe for a drink. Maybe for something else. He couldn't allow himself to think about what.

She led him to the left, through an elaborately molded archway into a sitting room decorated with antiques. They sat, side by side, on the tiny couch. He folded his hands in his lap. She did the same.

After a long moment, she spoke. "I've been waiting for that, Parker."

His heart lurched. "Waiting…for what?"

"For you to kiss me again." She glanced at him shyly, through the lace of her lashes. "I've been wanting you to kiss me again."

"I've, ah, I've kissed you after each date."

Her chuckle wreathed the room, warmed it. "Not like that." She leaned closer. "Not like this."

And then, to his shock and delight, she threaded her fingers into his hair and pulled his head down. Shivers rippled over his body, danced on his skin, as she kissed him. It was tentative and unskilled, and in that, it delighted him. She tasted him, tenderly, testing, lapping and licking. A nibble perhaps. All the while, she stroked his scalp, soothing him, caressing his nape and shoulders.

It was beyond excellent. It was miraculous.

The pain, which was never far away, dissolved completely and he was filled with an unfamiliar joy and... What was that? Peace?

By the time she drew back, he was aching, but it was a different kind of ache. A good ache.

He stared at her, taking in her shining eyes, her damp mouth, that riot of red curls haloing her head. Something odd filled his heart. Something he had never felt before. That peace was part of it, that bone-deep comfort when he looked at her, surely. But there was more. Raging desire, coiling panic and scorching determination to have her. Somehow, all these emotions swirled together in a unified surge, filling his heart and mind and soul.

And with a shock, he realized what it was, this thing he'd never felt before.

He loved her.

He *loved* her.

He would have sprung from the couch and dashed from the room—so terrifying was the prospect of loving anybody—if she hadn't entwined her fingers in his just then and said, in a matter-of-fact voice, "Shall we go upstairs?"

And so he couldn't spring from the couch and dash from the room—as his instinct for survival demanded—because all the blood rushed to his cock.

Perhaps every drop of it.

"Kaitlin..."

Her smile dimmed as he resisted the tug of her hand. "Don't you...want to?"

"Oh, God, yes. Yes. I want to. I haven't been able to think of much else for weeks."

She perked up at that. Glowed, perhaps. "Really?"

"Really. Sweetheart..." He flinched as he said the word, a word that really had no business between them. He covered his gaffe by pulling her into his arms and kissing her again. Showing her—he hoped—just how much he wanted her.

She was panting when he drew back. Her eyes were misty and her lips were damp.

"You see. I do."

"Then...why?"

He gestured to his chest, the scars lurking beneath his long-sleeved tee shirt. Always lurking. Always present. Burned into him. "I think you know."

"Parker..." she set her hand on his chest. Right where it ached most. Right were the bullet had ripped through him. Oddly, it didn't hurt. It usually always hurt. "Parker, it's okay. I don't mind about your scars."

He eased away. Hated that he eased away. "I do. I mind. I couldn't... I just couldn't... knowing you were looking at them." It was a little humbling, admitting his performance anxiety out loud. But she needed to know. A brilliant idea twined with his desperation. "We could turn off the lights..."

She shook her head. "I don't want to turn off the lights. I want to see you, Parker. I want to see your face. It's important for me to see your face."

He kissed her. On the forehead. "I would like very much to see your face too." And God, he would. As she came... It occurred to him that while she had pleasured him, he had not returned the favor. He vowed to do so. Sometime. Just not tonight—

"Then leave your shirt on."

He gaped at her.

"Leave it on." A smile quirked her lips and it blossomed mischievously. Her hand skated onto his thigh and then—*holy crap*—to his crotch. She cupped him. "This is what we really need bared, isn't it?"

Take her for the first time? Clothed? "I couldn't."

She laughed. "I'll keep my shirt on too."

What? He glanced at her breasts. His lip came out in a pout. "Where's the fun in that?"

"Whatever you want, Parker. Whatever makes you comfortable. It's fine with me. I just want..."

"What? What do you want?"

"You. Tonight. Now." The sincerity, the interest, the arousal, came off her in waves.

She was irresistible. Absolutely irresistible. A tsunami of lust swept his nervousness away.

She squeezed his cock.

He gulped. "Let's go upstairs." His voice cracked. He didn't even care.

CHAPTER NINE

Trepidation and arousal whipped through Parker as he followed Kaitlin up the stairs to her room. Though everything was a little blurry, on account of the pulse jerking in his left eye, he did notice that her bedroom was frothy and frilly, the bed festooned with lacy pillows. This did not calm his nerves.

She pushed all the pillows off the bed and then smiled at him.

His heart stuttered.

Lord almighty.

He glanced around, as though seeking escape. Which was insane. He didn't want to escape. He wanted...this.

She stepped closer. Took his hand in hers. Stroked his palm with her thumb. It comforted him. And then, guilelessly, she unzipped his jeans and knelt before him.

Fuck. He thought he was hard before?

Rolling down his briefs, she reached for him. And as much as he craved that...he stopped her. "Kaitlin..."

She looked up at him, her lips parted and glistening, her eyes wide. "Yes. Parker?"

"No."

Her expression dimmed. "No?"

Did she know her hand was moving? Stroking him? He nearly lost consciousness at the pleasure of that alone.

"I can't...I won't... I won't be able to last if you do that." And God, he wanted to last.

For some reason, his humiliating admission seemed to delight her.

She released him and sprang to her feet. "Okay," she said. "What would you like me to do?"

Myriad visions flooded his mind. He took a second to process them, to revel in this moment before he answered. "Take off your shirt." Yes. He needed to *see* her.

He'd always thought her shy and a little reserved, so it stunned him when she ripped off her t-shirt revealing her breasts, beautiful creamy mounds, cupped in a lacy pink bra.

His fingers twitched.

"What now?" Her grin was a little impish. He liked it, but it did not abate his nervousness.

"The-the bra."

She reached behind and undid the clasp, then let it fall.

His lungs locked. He stared. So perfect. Rounded and full, crested with rosy nipples. He licked his lips.

"Kaitlin…"

"What now?"

There was no reason for him to shake like this. He was a grown man. He'd been with a woman before, for heaven's sake. "Your jeans?"

She shimmied out of them in a rush. Kicked them off. They landed on the carpet on the other side of the room. She stood before him, naked, but for her panties. They were also pink, he noticed, in some part of his brain that was still working.

"Shall I get on the bed?"

His heart lurched. "I, ah, yes, please."

Now he knew she was teasing him, the way she sauntered away, hips waggling. The way she glanced at him over her shoulder.

Yeah, he was a grown man. He'd had a woman before. But he felt unaccountably like a virgin as she arranged herself on the bed, leaning against the headboard. She looked at him expectantly. "Are you going to join me?

His nod was jerky. He forced his feet to move—then realized he still wore his shoes, and his jeans were bunched around his ankles. Hastily, he yanked all that off and sat beside her, although being careful not to touch.

He wasn't sure why he was so careful not to touch, when it was the one thing his soul craved at the moment. He suspected it was his lingering fear. He tried to thrust it away, but failed.

So they sat, side by side on the bed.

He linked his fingers and studied them, unwilling to admit to her he wasn't quite sure what came next. He didn't want to screw this up. Didn't want to freak her out or try any of the crazy things he'd been dreaming of. So he said nothing. And didn't move.

After a while, she broke the silence, taking his hand in hers. At her touch, his confidence welled. "Parker, there's something you should know."

Damn. She was beautiful. He swallowed. "Okay."

"It's…it's been a while since I've done something like this."

Relief gushed through him. "It's been a while for me, too."

"How long?"

"Years. I had…a bad experience."

She blew out a breath. "Me too. I think I'm over it now. I think I'm ready now." She leaned a little closer.

He leaned a little closer as well. "I'm ready now too."

And he kissed her. It was a soft buss, a gentle exploration. But her lips parted and she welcomed him in, so it quickly became something more. He shifted toward her and cupped her cheek, holding her steady as he explored her mouth. After a moment, when he'd worked up the nerve, he took her breast in his hand and squeezed. Her nipple peaked against his palm. Her moan rumbled through him.

"Oh Kaitlin. Kaitlin," he murmured, working his way over her cheek to her neck, tasting her, nuzzling her, exploring the velvety skin. She shifted to give him better access, then fisted his hair to hold him at a spot that gave her pleasure.

Her response was invigorating, emboldening. He dipped his head and did the thing he'd been dreaming about for far too long. He drew her nipple into his mouth and sucked.

She arched into him, her moan a scintillating warble. He wanted to hear more.

Shuttling back and forth, he kissed and licked and nipped her breasts, drawing on her nipples until they became thick and swollen, until each touch made her wriggle and sigh. As he worked, he slid his hand lower, over her side, across her hips and into the warm juncture of her thighs.

She froze. Her breath hitched. He thought, perhaps, he'd moved too far, too fast, but then, ah then… she parted her legs.

Exhilaration swamped him.

She wanted this. She liked this.

He lifted his gaze and stared at her, taking in her expression as he lightly stroked her crease through the silk of her panties.

Her lips formed a tantalizing *O*. Her eyes glazed over. Her breath came out in pants.

"Do you like this?" he whispered.

"Oh yes. Please." Her legs parted more.

He took this as an invitation to slip beneath the silk. When he touched her, skin to skin, a little ball formed in his belly, and grew. She was wet. Hot. Ready.

He circled her clit, toying with it, dabbing at the underside and putting pressure on the swollen head. Slickness dampened his fingers. The musk of her arousal rose in the air.

His head swam. It had been so long for him. On the one hand, the urge to just lay her down and shove himself into her was strong. But he wanted to make this good for her. He wanted her to come—

Even as the thought occurred to him, she grabbed his arm in a brutal clutch and threw back her head and bellowed.

Bellowed.

Something about it, that feral sound, lit a fire in him. He yanked down her panties, settled between her legs, opened her with his thumbs, buried his face in her heat and tasted her.

Delight scoured him. She was sweet and delicious and heavenly. An angel.

A very aroused angel.

"Please, Parker. Please!"

He did not allow her surcease. He went on the attack, sucking and nibbling and tugging at her clit, eating her, devouring her. She writhed beneath him, grunting and groaning and muttering his name and imprecations and incessant pleas. She fisted his hair, wrapped her legs around his head, and thrust herself into him.

He gloried in it.

After she came the second time, he touched her again, this time with questing fingers, easing into her channel. He wanted to know, needed to know—

God. She was tight.

He shuddered; his cock surged in anticipation.

He pulled out—she whimpered—and he eased back in, with two fingers. She winced, wriggled a little, and then let out a sigh. "Ah, more."

He worked her, explored her as he sucked and lapped at her clit.

She stiffened. "Parker…"

"Mmm?"

"Par-ker!"

She'd been wet before. That was nothing compared to the flood raining down with this orgasm. She'd shivered and shook before. Nothing next to this orgasmic quake. She arched up on the bed, wrenching away from his touch altogether. The sound from her throat was guttural, insistent and tinged with desperation. Or bliss. He wasn't sure.

He was feeling both at the moment himself.

After she collapsed with a deep groan, he continued to stroke her gently, over the skin of her thighs, her belly, her arms, as she struggled for breath.

When she recovered, she perched up on her elbows and stared at him, her eyes filled with wonderment. At least, he hoped it was wonderment.

"Did you…like that?" he asked, hating the catch in his voice.

She blew out a laugh. "Like it? No."

His belly dropped.

"It was the most phenomenal thing ever. I loved it!"

He perked up at that. "Really?"

"*Ohmygod.* Parker!" She grabbed his face and yanked it to hers, kissed him brutally. "I had no idea it could be so—"

"So—?"

She leapt from the bed and spun in a circle, arms wide, hair flowing out behind her in a cloud. "Wonderful! Magnificent! Stupend—" She froze and then whirled to face him. "Can we do it again?"

He couldn't hold back the chuckle. "Most definitely."

"Oh, excellent." Her gaze landed on his cock.

Yeah. It was hard.

It bobbled at the mere caress of her attention.

Her smile blossomed. "But first…" she marched—naked—to the dresser and opened the top drawer. She pulled out a box and displayed it with a flourish.

Everything in him clenched when he realized what it was.

A box of condoms.

He nearly swallowed his tongue.

She came back to the bed, working the cellophane wrapping with her nails. It was resistant and she muttered beneath her breath. He took it from her as she plopped down beside him.

"I hope you don't think I'm too forward, buying these."

He snorted a laugh. "Not at all." Thank God she'd thought of it. He certainly hadn't.

She draped her arm around his shoulders and leaned against him as he worked the damn cellophane. That her breasts were pressed against his arm didn't help his concentration. And her perfume, whatever it was, besieged him. He struggled to focus. Finally, he got a corner up and ripped the plastic away.

"Are they the right size?" she asked, peeping up at him shyly.

He stared at her. His lips worked. *The right size?* Hell, he didn't know. It had been years since he'd bought a condom.

There were sizes now?

He tipped up the box and studied it. It was not forthcoming.

God, he hoped it was the right size.

His hands shook as he pulled a packet out and ripped it open. He resisted the urge to measure the latex sheath before he rolled it on. It fit. Relief gushed through him. He turned to her and forced a grin. "Size doesn't matter," he said. "Haven't you heard that?"

She giggled. "Yeah. That's what *he* said."

It was a joke, an awkward one, one that belied her nervousness. And somehow, the fact that she was edgy too, calmed him. He cupped her cheek and kissed her, calming them both, reminding them what they were about.

His cock needed no such reminding.

The knowledge that, in moments, he would be *in* her, raked him.

He stroked her breast as he nuzzled her lips, stroked her belly, her thighs, her hair. She melted in his arms, scooching down on the bed, pulling him with her until they both lay flat. He touched her clit. Rubbed it. She sighed and spread her legs. A welcome if he'd ever had one.

"Are you—are you ready?" he asked.

"Oh, yes," she said. And then she put her hands on his hips, as though to guide him.

He needed no such guidance, but hell, he would let her. He'd allow her anything in this moment.

He positioned himself between her legs and set his cock to her entrance. Nudged.

Heat scored him. Walked through him, dancing on his nerves and shimmering through his soul.

This was it.

This was the moment he'd been waiting—

"Parker." Her fingers tightened on his skin.

He froze. Looked down at her exquisite face, all bunched in a pout. "Yes, Kaitlin?"

"Just do it."

So he did.

He lunged. He sheathed himself in her.

It was heaven. Heaven and hell.

As he buried himself, her body reacted, tightening against his advance, shivering and rippling around him. He let go a low groan; it filled the room, twining with hers.

"Oh, yes," she sighed. "Yes."

He began to move, slowly at first because that was all he could manage. A pressure at the base of his balls, a tingling in his spine warned him he was close.

And so soon.

But damn. This was far too sweet to end so quickly.

He sucked in a breath and held back, moving in and out in a cautious slide, staring into her eyes. Her soul.

Her body responded, weeping for him, loosening a bit, quivering and sucking at him with each withdrawal. She wound her arms around him and stroked him over the fabric of his t-shirt. And oh, how he wished he hadn't insisted on wearing it. He so longed to *feel* her touch.

As though she understood, she fumbled beneath the hem and caressed him with flat palms, flesh to flesh as he worked away inside her. There was something hypnotic about her touch. Something soothing and, at the same time, energizing.

His passion rose. He increased his pace.

Her breath caught at a particularly fervent thrust and he stilled. He brushed back her hair and kissed her forehead. "Are you okay?" he asked.

"Yes." Not a whisper. A cry. "Yes. Please more like that."

His heart stuttered. "More like…what?"

"Hard."

Oh God.

He yanked out and plunged in…hard. Her body seized. He did it again and again and then, somehow, somewhere, he lost the reins. All of his dispassion, all of his reserve burned away in a conflagration of need and lust.

He went wild.

He knew he shouldn't. She was tiny and delicate and he needed to take care, but some untamed beast possessed him.

He went wild.

Sluicing in and out of her at a reckless pace, pummeling her, taking her, dominating her with his overwhelming need.

But she responded.

She took him. Took it all. And begged for more.

Something in his belly coiled into a tight ball. He changed his angle, lifted up a bit, lifted her with him, and thrust home, more deeply than he had reached before. She came. Clenching him with a heinous, slick fist. Writhing and screaming and then whimpering as her body collapsed.

He felt the insanity boil up, knew that it was upon him, the crisis he needed and dreaded in the same breath. He launched into a faster rhythm, something manic and crazed, something slightly out of control. He should have been horrified by his utter loss of restraint, but he had no time for that now. Now he needed… Now he wanted…

Yes.

Shards of bliss exploded, rocketing through him with mind-numbing speed, scraping at him and clawing at him and freeing him from the chains that had kept him bound for so long. He released. Released everything. The pain, the need, the desperation.

The loneliness.

All emptied from him in a torturous, blissful, boiling eruption.

Panting, he collapsed. He tried to collapse by her side, but missed and landed half on her.

She wrapped her arms around him and held him close, not letting him go. Not letting him retreat.

A blanket of warmth and delight clung to them. They shared breath and body heat and something more intangible in those moments, those moments after.

He lifted his head. Stared at her. This woman. This angel who had broken through all his walls. He stroked her cheek with a trembling fingertip. His heart contracted.

"Parker," she said on a breath. A prayer.

"Kaitlin."

There was nothing more that needed to be said.

Nothing.

CHAPTER TEN

Kaitlin lay in Parker's arms, limp. She couldn't move if the house was on fire.

Encased in cotton wool, her mind spun.

While she'd wanted Parker, dreamed and fantasized about connecting like this, merging physically with a man, with him, she'd never imagined it could be like this.

It had been perfect.

Physically pleasurable, certainly, but more. It was as though they'd touched on a soul-deep level.

She snuggled deeper into his arms, laying her cheek against the soft cotton covering his chest, breathing in his scent, listening to his heartbeat. His hold on her tightened. He made a noise, a murmur, a grunt, something that bespoke his contentment. But she felt it too, his delight. It soared around them, as though dancing on the ether, tangling with hers. Their auras tangled as well, the colors swirling together still, creating new colors, effervescent lights.

Perhaps that was what had made this, their first joining, so euphoric for her. The fact that she could feel his response, sense what he needed, and provide it for him. The give and take between them had been in seamless concert, a rapturous dance. She stroked him, eased him, soaking in his warmth. Nuzzling his neck, she tasted his peace.

A month ago she could never have imagined lying in a man's arms and wanting to stay there. To sleep there. As astonishing as it was, when she was with Parker, the buzz, the whispers and tumult of her gift, wafted away, leaving silence and serenity.

She loved it.

She suspected she might love him, but did not let herself dwell on that. It was far too new, this connection between them. But she didn't need to think. She didn't need to do anything. In this moment, it was enough to just...be.

Here. With him.

And then her belly growled.

His chest shook and she lifted her head to see a smile on his face. "Didn't you get enough to eat at the restaurant?" he asked.

She shrugged. "I guess I just wore off all those calories."

He kissed her. "You were magnificent."

"You were." Another kiss. And another. Until, all of a sudden, it was something more. His member, bare and damp—as he had pulled off the condom—rose against her thigh.

But he pulled away with a laugh. "We'd better get you something to eat." His expression took on a teasing light. "Do you have any chocolate pie?"

She giggled. Not just because he was teasing her about her voracious appetite for chocolate anything, but because, at the moment, she didn't have a craving for chocolate at all. Not a ping. She'd never *not* had a craving after a physical interaction with another person.

It was as though Parker had fed her.

Fed her soul.

Fed her soul chocolate.

"I don't have any pie at all."

He pushed out a lip.

"But I have soup. And cheese. And a jar of peanut butter."

His nose wrinkled.

"Some carrots."

"Carrots?"

"Bacon?"

He shook his head. "Do you want to go out?" he asked.

A ripple of unease nudged her. The comfort between them seemed to be escaping, like steam from a teakettle. His body was gathering tension even as they spoke, as though he were remembering his vulnerability and collecting his broken armor. She placed her palm on his chest and stroked him. He eased.

"No." She didn't want to go out. She didn't want to leave this room. "I'm really not hungry. Are you?"

"No."

"Can we stay here then? Like this?" She raked his scalp with her nails.

He looked down at her and their gazes tangled. The bond re-forged between them. Also, the heat. "Yes," he said. "I would like that."

He kissed her again, and this time, he didn't stop.

They did eat, but not until much later, not until Kaitlin had literally wrung him dry. Several times.

And it wasn't carrots or peanut butter. Parker ordered out and had his favorite Chinese restaurant deliver a collection of their best dishes. They sat, leaning against the sofa on her living room floor, laughing and chatting as they dined from little white containers.

He tried to teach Kaitlin how to use chopsticks, which resulted in much hilarity and dropped food, but in the end, she gave up and went to go get a fork.

When she returned, she handed one to him and Parker snorted. "It's not Chinese food unless you eat it with chopsticks."

She wrinkled her nose. And damn, she was cute when she wrinkled her nose. She was cute altogether, wearing an oversized football jersey that hung down to her knees...and nothing else. He'd pulled on his jeans, but only because he felt too exposed without them. She settled in by his side, warming him. "Well, if I use chopsticks, it's not food at all, because I won't get any in my mouth."

"I could feed you." He grabbed a slice of chicken with his chopsticks and held it to her lips. She opened and took it in. He watched, transfixed. And then, because he couldn't resist, he kissed her.

She laughed through the kiss.

"What?"

"Are you going to kiss me after each bite?"

"Maybe."

"Mmm. I might like this."

So he fed her that way.

The meal took a while. But neither of them minded.

Afterwards they cuddled on the couch, and kissed some more. And then she laid her head on his chest and rested. Slept, perhaps. And he held her. Just held her, stroking her hair, her back, her cheek. He loved this feeling. This peace. This oneness.

He thought, perhaps, this was what happiness felt like.

After a while her hand began to move over him as well. Nothing sexual or alluring; her caresses were as soothing and aimless as his. She stilled on his chest and fingered the lump, the ring under his shirt.

Though he wanted to pull her away, to distract her from that, he did not. When she lifted her head to look at him, he stiffened, preparing for the coming question.

"What is this?" she asked.

He drew in a breath. "My father's ring."

"Do you always wear it?"

"Yes."

"May I see it?"

He flinched. A little. But he pulled the chain out from beneath his shirt and handed it to her. She stilled as she touched it. Her expression went slack. And then she zeroed in on the scar on his cheek as though she *knew*.

It was foolish of him to leap to the conclusion that she'd seen the connection. That she recognized the design of the ring on his face. He was just super sensitive, is all. Always had been. No one else knew. They couldn't.

She wrinkled her nose and passed the ring back. "Why do you wear it all the time?"

"I wear it to remind me."

"To remind you of what?"

He caught her gaze, held it. "I wear it to remind me not to be like my father."

"I see."

"My father was…a very passionate man."

"Is that bad?"

"Passion can be destructive."

"Only if it is selfish passion."

He thought about that. Yes, his father's passion had been selfish. Selfish and demanding and overweening. And destructive.

She shifted so she could peer up at him, then kissed his face, far too close to his scar for comfort. "Do you want to talk about it?"

He shuddered. "Not really. Suffice to say, he was a violent man, when he was roused. And it didn't take much." At some point he needed to tell her everything. She deserved to know. But not tonight.

Thankfully she let it drop, nestling back in and curling against him. "I work with clients at the shelter who have run from men like that. Their stories are heartbreaking."

"I'm sure they are." His mother had tried running to a shelter. She'd grabbed Parker up one night and spirited him away. His father had found them and brought them home.

"I have one client now... She's in the shelter with her daughter. The little girl is three and her father threw her down the stairs."

"Fuck." Memory and agony twined in him. Acid curled in his gut. Parker's arms tightened around her as though he could stave off a memory, or a reality, or something.

"You should have seen this woman when she came in. Bruised, battered, spiritually crushed. It was horrible."

"No one should have to go through that." *No one.*

"And the father wants custody." She shivered. He stroked her hair to calm her. There was nothing more he could do. An odd and familiar urge rose in him—one he'd had often as a child—the wish that he was a super hero, someone strong and brave who could sweep in and save the day and make everything better. But he wasn't a super hero. He wasn't much of anything, really.

"The irony is, the father probably will get custody, because he's the one with the money. This woman has nothing." Kaitlin peered up at him. "Her husband is a bad man, Parker. He beat her. And then he beat her daughter. She needs a good divorce lawyer."

Parker heart swelled. "I'm a good divorce lawyer."

"She doesn't have any money."

Thirst for vengeance roiled through him. "We do *pro bono* work." Usually not for female clients, but they did it. "I'll help her."

"You will?"

"Of course I'll help her."

For Kaitlin.

And maybe for a little boy who was once beaten by a bad man.

* * *

He didn't have a chance to meet with her client during the following week because, according to Kaitlin, the woman was too nervous to leave the shelter, and it was against the rules for her to share the address. But he saw Kaitlin again several times the next week. Made love again each time, to Parker's delight—though each time with his shirt on, which he hated, but needed. He wanted to see her every night, all the time, but work intruded. His and hers.

On Monday night, he brought more take out—Italian this time—and they sat cross-legged on her carpet and ate in her living room, laughing at the antics of her new kittens, Boomer and Brandy, rescues she told him Emily had foisted upon her. And then he took her upstairs and made love to her again. On Tuesday, she had a client with an emergency and she called to cancel. It was stupid of him to sit on the deck of his Seattle apartment and stare out at the city and mope, but he did.

But he saw her on Wednesday.

On Thursday, he had to cancel. Barstow rushed into his office just as he was getting ready to leave, with ridiculous demands on a case that was going to court in the morning—things that should have been done weeks ago.

He called her with his regrets, but she sounded cheerful and patient.

"It's okay, Parker," she said in a perky voice. "We'll see each other tomorrow, right?"

"Yes." He'd have to console himself with the fact that tomorrow was Friday, and they'd made plans to meet at the island and spend the weekend together. But he wanted to be with her *now*.

The work that had once thrilled him, somehow seemed pallid and onerous. And, if he was honest, a little grimy.

All he'd ever wanted was to be a lawyer. To be someone important and powerful. It just seemed wrong to spend his days trying to cheat one party out of something due them, which, it felt, was what divorce lawyers did.

It had never bothered him before. He was a dispassionate bulldog, searching for a chink in a wall and then honing in on it like a heat seeking missile. But while he was working on Barstow's project, devising ways for Mr. Smithson to deny Mrs. Smithson a penny of alimony, despite the fact they'd been married for two decades and she had no visible means of support, well, it just felt wrong.

He supposed that was Kaitlin's influence.

This kind of work never bothered him, until the thought had entered his brain: *What would Kaitlin think of this?*

But it was his job. So he did it.

Like a bulldog.

He found the chink in Mrs. Smithson's armor, and exploited it.

And felt like shit.

Barstow loved it though. He clapped Parker on the back and chortled, "That's why I love you, Rieth. I can always count on you." And Parker's gut lurched.

Friday was looking better and better.

He practically hummed with anticipation all morning, whipping through work like a man on a mission. His headache came back, pinging in his neck and shoulders, but he forced himself to tolerate it, to relax.

He would see her soon.

Just the thought of her eased the tightness.

Around four he began tidying his desk. The ferry left at six, but it was a quick run from his Seattle office. He thought about leaving even earlier, but realized she wouldn't be there until the evening, so that might be a little too anxious on his part.

He had to chuckle at the thought.

He *was* anxious.

Far too anxious.

Still, excitement coiled in his belly as he stood and picked up his jacket. His suitcase was already in the car.

He was halfway to the door when the intercom buzzed. With a sigh, he returned to his desk and pressed the button on his phone. "Yes, Elaine?"

"Mr. Tucker is here to see you."

Parker frowned. *Shit.* He scrambled for his calendar. "Did he have an appointment?"

"I don't believe so, sir. But he's…" Her tone changed and Parker could tell she was whispering into the receiver behind her hand. "He's agitated."

Damn. Babysitting and hand holding. Just what he needed right now. It sucked that sometimes that was part of his job too. "Okay.

Send him in."

Tucker burst into the room. There was no other word for it. He was a tall, thickly muscled man with wiry hair and an abundance of frenetic energy. Every meeting Parker had had with him left him emotionally drained. As though he sucked the oxygen from the room.

"Rieth," he boomed. He always boomed. "I want to talk to you."

"Please, Mr. Tucker. Have a seat."

He didn't. He paced with a suppressed fury that made Parker a little dizzy. He finally halted before the window and propped his fists on his hips and, staring out at the city, snapped, "I am paying your firm a lot of money."

"Yes, sir."

"I expect a faster response."

"A...faster response?" Divorce proceedings were divorce proceedings. There was nothing fast about them.

"Finding them." He whipped around, his eyes were limned in red, nearly glowing with fervor. Parker clenched his jaw. He'd seen a look like that before. It never ended well. "I want my wife and daughter found. Brought back home. This delay is untenable."

Well, fuck. He was a lawyer, not a hound dog. "We have our best man on it."

Gilley was good. The best. But still, Parker couldn't help the ripple of trepidation at the thought of returning *anyone* to this man. The only reason he'd hired Gilley in the first place was because Barstow had insisted on it. *Every measure*, he'd said. *Every measure*.

"Your best man isn't good enough." Tucker slammed his fist into the wall. The pictures rattled.

Parker stared at the slightly dented spot. A hint of horror dribbled through him. He held himself as still as he could and sucked in a breath. "Sir, we try to help our clients wherever we can in these matters, but—"

"Oh, cut the bullshit, Rieth. Just tell me now if you're not good enough to handle this case and I'll find someone else."

Panic flared. "No. No. We can handle it, sir. I promise you."

"Find them."

"We will."

Tucker leaned in. His expression was fierce. His breath, sour. "You better," he spat. Then he wheeled and stomped for the door, yanking it open. He paused with his hand on the knob. "I'll give you a week. If they're not in my possession in one week, I'm dropping this firm. Is that understood?"

"Yes, sir."

Parker nearly collapsed when Tucker stormed off, but he couldn't. Because, in his wake, Barstow poked his head in the door. He didn't say anything, just shot Parker a speaking glance, but it was enough.

He sighed and trudged back to his desk to call Gilley. The last ferry left at eight pm. He could only hope he could reach his friend before then. Otherwise, he might not make it this weekend at all.

Damn, some days, he hated his job.

CHAPTER ELEVEN

Kaitlin arrived at the beach house late on Friday night. She was excited to see Parker, had really anticipated seeing him tonight, but had received a text that he'd hit a snag at work and wouldn't be here until tomorrow. While that stifled her mood, she was delighted to have some time with her friends. They didn't get to see each other nearly enough.

Riotous laughter rang off the walls as she dropped her suitcase by the door. She made her way down the hall, peering into the great room to see what was going on, but she couldn't see anything. The guys were all on their hands and knees on the floor, hidden by the fat sofa.

Kristi, who was in the kitchen making margaritas with Bella, greeted her with a wave.

Another round of male chuckles rumbled and Kaitlin went up on her toes to see what the guys were doing. They were all perched in a circle around a man lying on the floor, tall and well-muscled with dark skin and a handsome face—with his head on a scale. Her heart leapt. "Patrick is here," she sighed as Kristi wrapped an arm around her and rubbed her back. Kristi had such calm energy. She never minded a hug from her.

"Umm hmm," Kristi responded. "He just got in."

Bella sidled up next to her but was careful not to touch. "He's on leave."

Kaitlin let out a breath. "Thank God he's back." She hated it when Patrick went away. Sure, it was his job to go to Afghanistan or

96

Iraq or Colorado. But she hated when he was gone. He'd always been like a big brother to her...more. Her champion. Her protector. Her confidant.

Patrick hefted himself to his feet and peered at the scale. "Twenty two," he said.

Drew chortled as Cam lay down in Patrick's place.

"What are they doing?" Kaitlin asked.

Bella sighed. "They're weighing their heads."

"Weighing their heads?" What on earth for?

A shrug. "So far Drew's winning."

"He would." Kristi smirked. "The fathead."

Patrick glanced up and let out a whoop. "KK!" he cried. "You're here!" He nearly stepped on Cam as he sprinted across the room. He certainly ignored Cam's howl. He swept Kaitlin up in a huge bear hug and swung her around. "Baby girl, aren't you a sight for sore eyes."

She put her hand on his cheek and stared up at him. His aura was a little cloudier, but not too bad. And the shadows in his eyes wafted away as he grinned at her. She and Patrick had always been close. Probably because, unlike the rest of their friends, they'd both experienced the prejudices of the world. Patrick, because he was a very large and intimidating-looking black man—which was ridiculous because he was the sweetest man on the planet—and Kaitlin, because of her gift. When people learned about it, they either recoiled or they came at her with avaricious zeal, wanting to know next week's winning lottery numbers or to speak to dead relatives.

She adored Patrick. And good heavens, she'd missed him. He'd been the star running back in college and had played pro for a while before he decided to enlist in the Air Force and pursue his dream as a pilot.

"How are you, Patrick?"

"Good. I'm good."

She ignored the lie and hugged him again, surrounding him in a soothing cloud.

"God, I've missed that," he huffed.

"Me too."

The other guys came to greet her as well, giving her quick hugs and busses to the forehead. All but Drew. His hug was longer. It always was.

She pulled away and patted him on the chest. "How are you

doing, Drew?"

He shrugged. Then frowned at her. "Why haven't you answered my calls?"

"Oh, it's been really busy at work." She made a great show of removing her sweater and arranging it on the back of the chair. She couldn't meet his eye, or he might sense the lie. Drew was pretty clueless about most things, but he was pretty good at ferreting out a lie.

She really didn't want to have the conversation she knew was coming, so she sloughed it off with a chipper, "So what's everyone been up to?"

They all gathered around the table and ate nachos and drank Margaritas as they got caught up. Kristi and Cam sat together, fingers linked, and Bella and Holt were side by side as well. Kaitlin made it a point to sit by Patrick, leaving the only spot open between Cam and Bella, much to Drew's consternation. He practically pouted.

Kaitlin ignored him.

Before, she would have tried to make an effort to calm him, or send him a smile or something, but that felt wrong to her somehow. As though she'd be giving him encouragement.

It created a tension between them, of course, his pushing in and her pushing back, sizzling where their trails touched.

Fortunately, everyone else was oblivious. They all sipped and crunched and chattered on gleefully. Which was nice. Kaitlin hated drama, and she certainly didn't have the energy for it now.

Parker had exhausted her—several times this week. But it wasn't a negative kind of exhaustion, as she'd experienced before after raw physical contact. It was sweet. And satisfying. It surprised her to realize she hadn't had a chocolate binge all week.

"Why are you grinning like that?" Patrick whispered in her ear.

She shot him a look. Ah, Patrick. *He* wasn't oblivious. "I'll tell you later," she whispered back.

He nodded and slipped his arm around her shoulders and pulled her into a quick little half hug. At which, Drew frowned.

Again, she pushed his annoyance away.

Honestly. Sometimes it was a pain in the butt to feel *everything*.

She focused instead on the chatter around the table. Bella was excited to report that her sex toy shop had record sales last month since Holt had started referring her to his friends and Cam had upgraded her website.

"Upgraded?" Cam snorted. "I would call it a complete overhaul."

Kristi smacked him.

"What? Well, it was."

Bella frowned. "Okay. The website was shit. I admit it."

"We monetized it, upgraded the cache and, for God's sake, changed the operating system."

Kaitlin laughed. "I have no idea what any of that means."

"It means," Bella said, rubbing her hands together, "I'm making money."

Holt tugged her closer. "It means, she won't lose the store."

"Were you going to lose the store?" A trickle of chagrin swept through her. How had she missed that?

Bella shrugged without answering. Which meant: *Yes.*

"How are things at Beanies?" she asked Kristi. Kristi and their friend Lucy owned a coffee shop in the Montlake neighborhood of Seattle.

Before Kristi could answer, Bella snorted. "It's Montlake. It's coffee." And everyone laughed. Between the University of Washington and all the tech companies located nearby, there was always a need for a jolt of caffeine.

"And how about you Patrick? How was your tour?" She patted his knee.

She did not expect his flinch. A scorching tendril flowed up her arm and into her heart and mind, filling her with a jumble of visions. None of them pleasant.

Firefights. Flames. Explosions.

A crash.

Patrick holding the hand of a young airman…as the boy died.

Immediately, she regretted the question.

Why had she not seen that too?

"I'm sorry," she said softly.

"It's okay. He squeezed her hand and turned to the rest of the group. "I'll be honest. It was a rough tour. One of the worst. I'm, ah, thinking about retiring."

A chorus rounded the table, but Patrick lifted his hand and they all silenced. "It was a good run. I accomplished what I thought I needed to do. But now… Now I think I'm ready for some peace and quiet."

Probably mostly peace.

"What will you do?" Cam asked.

"Football?" This from Holt.

Patrick cracked a smile. "I'm too old for football."

"Hardly…"

"Too beat up then. I was thinking about maybe flying for a commercial carrier or something."

Yes, he would be good at that. And Kaitlin would appreciate having him closer. She would appreciate knowing he was safe. She nodded. "You could still fly, travel—"

"Pick up stewardesses." Everyone threw their balled up napkins at Drew. "What? Don't tell me it didn't cross your mind."

Patrick chuckled. "Okay. Yeah. It did."

"Hah! I knew it."

"I think that's a good idea, Patrick," Kaitlin said. She nibbled her lip. "But not the stewardess part."

Laughter rocked the room.

A blanket of darkness cloaked the view of the ocean, but Kaitlin could still hear it as she sat on the deck with her eyes closed. She'd needed to come out here, for a moment alone.

That is to say, away from Drew.

She loved him, but his approaches were becoming uncomfortably insistent. Almost desperate. So, when the guys went downstairs to play a game of pool and Bella and Kristi went to take a soak in the hot tub, she came out to the deck to sit in the shadows.

The rustle of the wind in the trees tangled with the croaking bullfrogs. The shush of the waves and the scent of brine danced on the breeze.

She allowed her mind to wander.

It wandered to Parker.

This was not a surprise.

She'd been replaying all their dates, all their interactions, especially their sexual interactions, over and over in her mind. She'd been reviewing her feelings for him. Incessantly.

In all that she just simply knew some things without even trying, no matter how she looked at this or meditated on this or prayed about this, the answers were muddled.

Oh, her feelings for him were clear.

She was head over heels. That part was easy. But she didn't know how he felt—really felt—and she didn't have a clue if being with him was the right choice.

It seemed right. But lots of things seemed right, when they weren't.

If only the universe would be more clear. Send her a lightning bolt or a neon sign or a carrier pigeon with the message, *yes! Parker is the one. Your soul mate. The man for you.*

But other than that flutter of her heart when she thought of him, that pang of longing when they were apart, and the absolute delight when he touched her—nothing.

She didn't like being clueless, she found.

Perhaps she should be more sympathetic to her clueless friends in the future.

The slider opened and she stiffened.

"Hey there KK," Patrick's low voice enrobed her and she relaxed. "Are you hiding?"

She laughed. "Maybe a little."

"May I join you?" He held up two steaming mugs. "I brought cocoa."

"Oh. Cocoa!" She reached for one of the mugs but he held it back. "Not this one," he winked. "This one is laced with whiskey. This one's mine."

She took the drink he offered and took a sip. Delicious. "Thanks."

How Patrick knew she needed this, right now, was a mystery.

He slipped into a chair and settled his gaze on her. "Something's different about you," he said.

"Mmm." She took another sip. "I met someone."

He shot her a surprised glance. "As in, a man?"

She nodded, biting back her grin at his surprised tone.

Patrick was the only one, of all of her friends, who knew the truth about what had happened that night so long ago in college. He'd been home when she and Emily had returned, clothes ripped, eyes wild. He'd comforted them. And then, of course, he'd vowed to exact revenge. Both Emily and Kaitlin had insisted he let it drop.

Patrick was the only one who knew how deeply the incident had wounded Kaitlin. Only Patrick knew she'd responded by locking herself away.

He took a snort of his cocoa-whiskey and cleared his throat. "Is it serious?"

"I think so."

"Does Drew know?"

Kaitlin frowned at him. "Drew knows I met him."

"Does Drew *know?*"

Kaitlin sighed.

Patrick scrubbed his face. "Baby girl, you gotta tell him."

"I know."

"You gotta tell him he doesn't stand a chance. That guy is tail over arse in love with you."

She sighed again. He was right. Really right. Drew deserved to know. But, *good gravy*, she didn't want to have that conversation.

"So, tell me about this guy."

"What guy?" Kristi padded up behind Patrick with a towel around her waist, picked up his mug and took a sip. She grimaced. "Shit, Patrick. Is there any cocoa in there?"

He grinned. "Not much."

"I guess. So what guy are we talking about?"

Patrick glanced at Kaitlin with a question in his eyes. *Tell her or prevaricate?* It said.

Kaitlin shrugged. They'd all know soon enough. She was spending the rest of the weekend at his place...if he ever made it. "I met a guy."

Kristi thudded into a chair and stared at Kaitlin in shock.

"A *man?*"

Kaitlin shot a frown at Patrick. "Why does everyone ask if it's a man?"

"Because you never date."

"You never dated. Like not once. We all thought..." Kristi let the sentence trail away.

"You thought, what?"

Patrick and Kristi exchanged a look. A telling look. The universe whispered in her ear. It was laughing.

"You thought I was a lesbian?"

"Kinda?"

"Oh my." Kaitlin huffed a chortle. "No. No. But you know men...touching...is difficult for me."

"Right. I just never realized it was *that* difficult. I mean..." Kristi leaned in. "No sex?"

"None."

"Not once?"

Kaitlin shook her head. Then stilled. Not true. Not anymore. A smile curled her lips.

"So who is this guy?" Patrick asked. He had *that* tone, that protective rumble.

"His name is Parker."

"Parker?" Kristi nearly screeched. "The guy who's friends with Ash...the guy who dumped Emily?"

"Wait. Some guy dumped Emily?" Patrick's fingers curled.

"It's okay." Kaitlin patted his bulging forearm. "They're okay. And they're seeing each other now." She shot a frown at Kristi. Patrick did tend to go into caveman mode when anybody dissed his girls. It occurred to her they needed to find him a woman of his own to fret over. "And yes. Parker is Ash's friend."

Patrick's fierce expression did not ease. "I don't think I like this guy."

"You will like him." Not a hope or a suggestion. A command. "He's coming this weekend, so you'll get to meet him." She sent him a serious look. "Be nice."

"I'm always nice."

Both Kaitlin and Kristi snorted.

"I am."

"So, tell me about him," Kristi said.

Kaitlin sighed. "Well, he's tall and handsome."

"Umm hmm." Patrick was not convinced.

"He's a lawyer."

He waggled his head. "Better."

"And so nice..." She trailed off.

"Baby girl, I am sensing some worry in your tone."

"Worry?"

"Yep."

"Well...I've never been in a relationship before. I've never felt like this before. I suppose I am a little scared."

Kristi nodded. "It is scary."

"I mean, what if it...goes sour?"

Patrick stroked his mug with a thumb. "You said it's serious."

Kristi gasped. "You said it's serious?"

"Yes. Very."

He laughed and shrugged a muscled shoulder. "Then... So?"

"What do you mean?"

"So what if it goes bad. It also goes good. At least for a while. Right?"

"I suppose."

"Enjoy it while it's good, baby. My momma always said..." He affected a strong Southern accent. "Don't go borrowing trouble from tomorrow, honey child."

Kristi laughed. "Your momma said that?"

"She surely did."

Kaitlin snorted. "I can't imagine your momma saying it in *that* tone of voice." His mom had gone to Princeton.

"Well, she did."

"In that tone of voice?"

"In exactly that tone of voice. But the tone of voice doesn't matter as much as the sentiment. If you like this guy, KK, you gotta snatch him up. Or else some other good woman will."

"And if it doesn't last?"

"How do we ever know what's going to last?" Kristi asked.

Patrick lowered his lashes. "Word."

The sudden downward spiral of his energy concerned Kaitlin. She put her hand on his, sending him positive vibes, and focused her attention on Kristi. "Do you think you and Cam are going to last?"

"If I have anything to say about it." She grinned. "But that's not the point. Cam and I took a risk getting involved..."

"How so?"

"We took the risk of getting hurt, or pissing everyone off, or ruining what we have here. But we did it, because the prospect of walking away from each other—away from something that could *mean* something, something that could change both our lives in a really amazing way—was far riskier." Kristi shivered and pulled her towel more tightly around her. "In this game, when you lose, it sucks. But when you win...there's nothing like it."

"I'm looking forward to meeting this guy, KK—"

"I'm looking forward to it too, Patrick."

"But I gotta say it. If I don't like him, ain't nobody gonna wonder about it."

Kaitlin grinned. "I wouldn't expect anything less. But you will like him. I promise."

"I better." He sighed and leaned forward and kissed her forehead. "Now Kristi and I gotta go inside."

Kristi blinked. "We do?"

"We do." Patrick tipped his head toward the house. "Drew's coming. And Kaitlin has something to tell him." He squeezed her hand for reassurance. It didn't help.

As Patrick and Kristi went inside, Drew came out, grunting a greeting to them as they passed.

He set his beer on the table as he sat down. He stared at her for a long while before he spoke. "Kaitlin, I need to talk to you."

"I need to talk to you too, Drew—"

He ignored her. "What the hell is going on with you? You seem…different."

She suppressed a smile. For Drew to notice anything that wasn't on fire was a huge step. But this wasn't going to be a fun conversation for either of them.

"There is something different, Drew. And I want to tell you about it."

"Is it that *guy*?" He spat the word, the way one might say *serial killer* or *vegetables*.

She nodded.

"I knew it. But listen, Kaitlin—"

"Drew." She put her hand on his. Felt his fear, his angst. She sent him a trail of peace, praying for his acceptance. "This guy is it for me."

Yes. He was. She'd realized the truth of it. No matter what he felt for her. No matter what happened or didn't happen between them. He was it.

Aside from the fact she'd never had feelings like this for a man before, aside from the fact it was delightful to finally be able to touch someone without pain—he was, simply said, the most wonderful, courageous, amazing person she'd ever met.

Drew paled. His hand went cold. "It? As in *it*, it?"

She smiled. "It, it. I know you have feelings for me. And I know you have for a long time—"

"I do, Kaitlin. I lo—"

She couldn't let him say it. "But Drew. It's not meant to be. Us. Please understand. You are incredible. Cute. Funny. Sexy."

His blush rose. "You think I'm sexy?"

"You're very sexy. But you're not the one for me and…" She shrugged. "I'm not the one for you."

"But, Kaitlin—"

"Drew." She silenced him with a look, let it speak for her. He knew her. He'd known her forever. He knew she was rarely, if ever wrong. And he knew she was stubborn when she needed to be. "Just, no."

He gaped at her, a shattered expression on his face. After a long moment, he said, "You're sure about this?" His jaw clenched. His eyes shined suspiciously.

"Very sure. As sure as I've ever been."

He blew out a breath and stood, turning his back to her, leaning against the rail, staring out toward the hidden sea. He might have dashed at his cheeks.

Her heart clenched. "One day you'll see. You'll meet someone and it will be perfect and you'll see."

He burbled a laugh. "Any idea when I might meet this *perfect woman?*" He threw out his arms, and yelled into the shadows, "Where the hell is she?"

Kaitlin shook her head, though he wasn't paying attention. His body, his awareness, was angled away. "One day. When you're both ready." She joined him at the rail and gently rubbed his back, ignoring his flinch. "You'll find each other," she whispered, "I promise."

"Aw, shit, Kaitlin." He whirled and tugged her into a hug, burying his damp face in her shoulder. She held him and patted him and enrobed him in what she hoped was an inspirational cloud. "I thought… I really thought…"

"I know." More pats. "I know."

He yanked back and frowned at her. "I hope you're happy with this guy." His tone was fierce. She would have thought him angry, if she hadn't known him so well.

"I hope so too."

"If he hurts you, I swear, I'll break him in half."

She chuckled. "I'll be sure to let him know."

"And if you ever, ever change your mind—"

"I won't."

"But if you do, ever… I'll be here waiting."

"Thank you, Drew," she said. But in her heart she knew it wasn't true. He wouldn't be waiting long at all.

CHAPTER TWELVE

Parker was nervous as he took the ferry ride to the island on Saturday, and not just because Gilley reported he'd hit a snag in the search for Tucker's wife. But because he'd received a text from Kaitlin. A horrifying one. It said: *My friends can't wait to meet you.*

Why the prospect made him shudder and lose all appetite for food, he wasn't sure. He'd met a few of her friends. Spent a lovely day with Holt and Emily not catching any fish. They both seemed very nice, even Holt, despite his intimidating exterior.

He'd met Drew too. Once. On the ferry.

Parker hadn't cared for his possessive attitude. He suspected the hardest part of the day would be meeting Drew. And not choking him. Or getting choked.

But Parker knew how close Kaitlin was with this group of friends. Over their many dates, she'd shared stories of their adventures in college, and after. He'd seen her fondness for them in her eyes, heard it in her tone.

If the two of them were to have something lasting, he knew he needed to win their acceptance.

So he was a little nervous.

Okay, scared shitless.

When the ferry docked he sent her a text and she responded. *We're at the house,* she said. *Come on by.*

Shit.

He stopped by Ash's place and dropped off his stuff first. He thought about making a drink to calm his nerves and then decided it might not be wise. He definitely wanted to be on top of his game. He had to make a good impression.

His feet felt like lead as he trudged over to the house next door. It belonged to Lane Daniels, but Kaitlin explained they all co-leased it and traded off weekends. The only saving grace in all this was that *all* of them wouldn't be there today.

Just so things could be crappier, Drew opened the door to his knock. He gave Parker the once over, a slow up and down rake of a glance. His lip curled. He didn't budge. Didn't welcome him in or anything.

Parker cleared his throat. "I'm Parker. Kaitlin's friend?"

Drew grunted and turned, storming back down the hallway, bellowing, "He's here." Which was concerning.

But he left the door open.

Parker took this as a welcome. An invitation, of sorts. And he followed.

The house was laid out a lot like Ash's, though much smaller, with a great room flanked by floor to ceiling windows overlooking the ocean, and an open kitchen and dining area to the left. As he entered, three large men stood.

Holt nodded in greeting, but the other two folded their arms over their chests and stared at him, in concert with Drew. The taller one, a muscled African American, with a tattoo of a screaming eagle on his bulging bicep, narrowed his eyes.

Silence spat through the room. Acid snarled in his gut. Parker stiffened his spine.

He felt like a lone soldier facing a battalion.

Or a guy meeting his girl's parents for the first time.

But he could do this.

"Hi guys," he forced out in the cheeriest tone he could manage. His voice hardly cracked at all. "I'm here for Kaitlin."

Drew's muscles bunched. He growled.

Parker winced and reworded his ill-formed declaration. "I'm here to see Kaitlin."

"Sit down," the black guy suggested, though it wasn't much of a suggestion. More like an order.

Parker sat. He took the easy chair by the sliding glass door, certain it wasn't a decision based on his well-honed survival instincts. The bristling men all sat on the sofas facing him. That the four of them sat in concert, like the Borg, was not comforting in the slightest.

That they said nothing, merely studied him, was even more nerve-wracking. He glanced around, a desperate search for Kaitlin. Where was she?

"So," Holt said.

"So…"

"So…"

"So…"

All of them. One after the other. As though they'd rehearsed or something.

Ye Gods.

The guy with the tattoo leaned forward. "You're dating our Kaitlin."

Not a question. Not in any way shape or form, but Parker nodded.

"She's…very special to us."

"I understand that. She'd told me a lot about you guys and—"

Drew leapt to his feet and raked his fingers through his spiky hair. "If you hurt her, we'll hunt you down like a dog."

"Drew." Holt's warning was low, growled.

"Well, we will," Drew snapped.

"We will," the enormous black guy offered in a smooth, calm voice. He shot Parker an assessing look. "But I think he knows that."

"I do." Parker nodded. "I know you all care for her—"

"Damn straight," Drew snorted.

"So do I."

Silence sizzled for a long moment. Then Holt asked, in a deceptively soft voice, "Are you serious about her?"

Parker's heart jerked, then pounded. He was. Oh, God, he was. But he hated exposing his private feelings to all of them. It was, of course, the only way.

"Very serious. She's…unlike anyone I've ever met."

"You do realize she's *special.*" This from Drew, who spat the word.

"Drew." The black guy frowned.

"Well goddamn it, Patrick. He's got to know."

"Of course." Parker tried not to sound offended, but it was tough. She *was* special. The most amazing woman he'd ever met. It changed him, in some indefinable way, being with her. She made him a better man. The man he longed to be. Brave and funny and...loveable.

But he couldn't say all that.

Patrick leaned forward again, his muscles bunching, the eagle on his arm seemed to reach out it's talons as he moved. "And what are your intentions?"

"My...intentions?" He garbled a laugh. "Are you asking if I want to marry her?"

Holt straightened, pinned him with a sharp glance. "Do you?"

Parker froze. He's never dreamed of marriage, never dared. The thought scared him to death. Overwhelming passion and emotion had nearly killed him once. He'd vowed to divorce himself from such drama. To hold himself apart.

And he'd been a raging success at that.

Until Kaitlin.

But marriage?

He decided to tell the truth, or a part of it. It was prevarication, and he knew it. But a declaration at this point was ludicrous. "It's a bit early for that..." Drew relaxed a bit. "But I can't think of anyone I'd rather spend my life with."

Holt nodded and stood. He strode toward Parker with his hand outstretched. "That's good enough for me."

"Seriously?" Drew burbled.

"Me too." Patrick offered a hand as well.

"Are you freaking kidding me?"

"Me too." The other guy, the one who hadn't spoken yet, joined in. "I'm Cam, by the way," he said.

"Cam." Parker shook his hand.

They all turned to Drew. Parker had the sense this was the handshake that mattered most. Drew put his fists on his hips. "I thought we were going to grill him."

Patrick chuckled. "We did."

"That?" Drew waved at Parker. "That was grilling? Seriously? You boys have lost your touch. He's a friend of Ash Bristol's for fuck sake. Remember him? The guy who broke Emily's heart?"

"Yeah, well," Holt crossed into the kitchen and pulled out a couple beers. He popped off the tops and handed one to Parker. He didn't really want a beer, but he took it. "Ash and Emily are dating now."

Drew's eyes bugged out. He threw up his hands. "What the fuck is happening around here?" he muttered as he clomped out onto the deck.

Patrick sidled up next to Parker and clapped him on the back. "You need to give Drew some time. This is tough for him."

Cam nodded. "He's been in love with her for years."

Parker's muscles bunched. Something nasty slithered through him. "For years?"

"Chillaxe, dude," Cam snorted a laugh. "He's been after her for years…and they're not together. Think about it."

Okay. There was that. Parker let himself relax. He took a swig of beer.

It was all good, he reminded himself. He'd faced his greatest fear—meeting her protectors—and they hadn't killed him. That was promising. Maybe it would all work out.

"Is…Kaitlin here?"

Holt rolled his beer between his palms and nodded. "The girls all took a walk on the beach."

Patrick laughed. "KK didn't want to go. We made her."

Um…*KK*?

Parker shot a look at the intimidating guy. Yeah, even when he wasn't frowning and glowering, he was pretty intense. "Patrick, what do you do for a living?" If he had to guess, he'd go for *Gladiator* or some shit.

"I…am in the Air Force."

"Ah." That made sense. He had a military vibe about him.

"Holt's an architect, Cam's a programmer and Drew…" He gestured out to the deck where Drew was scouring the beach with an eagle eye. "He's a fire fighter."

Right. Parker remembered that little tidbit from the ferry. A fire fighter. A true hero. And he was in love with Kaitlin.

Awesome.

Cam tipped up his beer. "He's stationed over on the Eastside. Comes from a family of firemen."

Of course. Parker wondered where Drew had left his cape.

"And you?"

"Lawyer."

This seemed to appease them, this proof that he could provide for their…*daughter*. He tried not to laugh at the thought. It was probably far too early to laugh. Or joke. Or let down his defenses.

But he'd survived it. The worst was over. He tipped back his beer. The one he hadn't wanted. Somehow it was empty.

Holt glanced at the beach. "I think I see the girls coming." He shot a grin at Parker. "Are you ready for round two?"

His pulse jolted. "Round two?"

Patrick snickered. "You thought this was tough?"

Cam laughed. "Yeah, just wait."

"Here you go, buddy." Holt shoved a full beer into his hand. "You're gonna need this."

Kaitlin rushed up the stairs ahead of everyone else, her heart pounding, her breath in pants. She could feel Parker's panic. Had felt it out on the beach. An unfamiliar anger rose in her breast—anger at her friends.

She knew the guys wanted to vet him. She knew they wanted to protect her. They'd insisted—*insisted*—she go for a stupid walk on the beach. But Parker was *hers*. He was a tender soul, a wounded man, and she couldn't bear to see him hurt even more.

Rounding the top of the stairs, her gaze fell on Drew, standing on the deck. His bristling colors were unmistakable.

Her stomach lurched.

Oh. Good. Gravy.

What had they done?

She pushed past him and burst into the house. And stopped.

Two things froze her in her tracks. The first was that Holt, Cam, Patrick and Parker were laughing. *Laughing.*

The second was the sight of Parker himself. She hadn't seen him for two days. Had she forgotten how handsome he was? Her heart lifted, sang.

He saw her and stilled. A slow smile tweaked his lips.

She skipped across the room and into his arms. And heaven. It was heaven being in his arms. He closed them around her and squeezed. Odd that. It felt like he was reassuring *her*.

"Kaitlin," he said. "I missed you."

"I missed you too."

He pulled back and kissed her. Nothing very lurid, just a sweet tease. The brush of his lips on hers. They did have an audience, after all. Kaitlin could feel their energy swirling around her. She ignored it and grabbed Parker by the ears and pulled him back. Kissed him fully, infusing all her want and need and adoration into it.

"Ahem." Holt.

Damn Holt.

Parker chuckled a little and eased her away, but then, as though he couldn't resist, he pressed his lips to her forehead. "How've you been?" he asked.

"Good. And you?"

"Busy."

"I missed you."

"I missed you too."

"You already said that." This from Drew, who had, apparently followed her inside.

The room erupted then as Kristi and Bella tromped in, laughing and chattering and stomping the sand from their shoes. When their gazes fell on Parker, the hubbub evaporated.

They stared at him as though he were an exhibit at the zoo. He shifted from one foot to the other.

"Everyone," Kaitlin gusted. "This is Parker."

"This is Kristi."

"Hi, Parker."

"And her sister, Bella."

"Hey."

An uncomfortable silence settled.

"Shall we all sit?" God bless Patrick. Kaitlin smiled at him and he winked.

Oh good. A wink was good. It meant Patrick approved.

Or at least, he didn't disapprove.

They took their places at the table and Holt brought around more beer, though Parker declined. Once they settled in, all gazes, once more, drifted to him. His aura pulsed. He seemed like a man awaiting execution.

"So," Patrick said. "Parker's a lawyer."

"Humph." Bella crossed her arms. "A lawyer?"

Parker nodded. "For Barstow and Rank."

Kristi frowned. "Barstow and Rank?" She glanced at Cam. "Isn't that the firm that represented Lane in the divorce?"

"Lane Daniels? Yes." From the way Parker leapt on that tidbit, Kaitlin suspected he thought that was something, a way to bond with this group. *Not so much.* While the guys all nodded and murmured, the women glowered.

She set her hand on Parker's. Laced her fingers with his. "Both Lane and Lucy are our friends," she said softly.

The divorce had not been amicable.

In the slightest.

Everything had gone in Lane's favor.

And Kristi was Lucy's best friend.

"Oh. Ah. I see. It wasn't my case." He didn't say it, but Kaitlin felt his thoughts. Mentally, he added, *Thank God.*

Kristi picked at the label on her beer. "Lawyers aren't very nice people."

Parker flinched.

Kaitlin squeezed his hand. "Parker is nice."

Bella squinted her eyes, as though trying to *see* this juxtaposition.

"He's representing one of my clients at the shelter."

Kristi nibbled her lip. "At the shelter?" Kristi had done work at Boudicca as well. She understood. Women in the shelter were there for a reason. Usually a very bad reason. She studied Parker with an assessing eye.

"Yes." Kaitlin rubbed his arm. *"Pro bono."* She sent him a smile. He smiled back. Neither of them cared that no one else spoke for a while. Or perhaps they were speaking. They just missed it.

"So what about his choice in friends?" Bella said. She said it loudly enough to break through their private bubble.

"What?" Kaitlin snapped.

Bella's eyes widened. Because Kaitlin never snapped. "Ash Bristol? The douche. Devlin Fox?"

Annoyance raged through Kaitlin's chest. "Emily and Ash have worked things out. You know that Bella. And it's hardly Parker's fault that Devlin wrote a bad review of Tara's bakery—"

Parker started. "Devlin wrote a bad review of Tara's bakery?"

Kaitlin nodded. "Three burps."

"Wow. That's funny." Parker chuckled. Actually chuckled.

Kristi leaned in. She looked like she wanted to go on the warpath. "Why is that so funny?"

Parker shrugged. "Because he's kind of got a crush on her."

Holt and Bella exchanged a glance, but kept silent. They knew something. Kaitlin made a note to grill them for the goods later. But for now, all she could think about was getting Parker alone. And maybe jumping his bones.

He was still very tense, but she knew a way to relax him.

"I agree with KK," Patrick said. "You judge a man by his actions. Not on other people's merits."

She shot him a triumphant smile. "Exactly. Thank you Patrick."

"I don't know," Drew put in. "I think friends are a measure of the man." He glared at Parker who, to his credit, didn't respond. Kaitlin tightened her hold on him. Her fingers were nearly white. "You got one guy who seduces little girls—"

"Emily is hardly a little girl. She's a grown woman," Kaitlin lunged to her feet and snapped.

Drew stood as well. His voice rose, as though to drown her out. "One guy who destroys businesses with his bitter diatribes, and the other guy—what's his name—with the ascot…"

"What about him?" She shouldn't have roared, but seriously. Drew was pissing her off.

Drew's lips flapped. "He wears a freaking ascot!" A bellow.

"Andrew Boone. Enough. Let it drop. I told you last night—"

A sudden shift in the energy to her right, an odd cool waft from Parker, stopped her reprimand mid-sentence. She turned to Parker. His eyes were locked on Drew, his face ashen.

"Parker?" she whispered. "What is it?" Though when she touched his shoulder, she knew. *Visions of licking flames, sensation of heat and pain. A cloak of fear.*

And then, a man appeared, fighting through the mists of terror.

A hero.

Parker swallowed, a jerky undulation of his throat. "Your name is Andrew Boone?"

"Yeah." Drew clipped. "What of it?"

"And you're a firefighter?" This, he croaked.

"Yeah."

"Were you-were you named after your father?"

Drew frowned. "Yeah."

"Was…your father a firefighter too?"

Drew's gaze narrowed. "Yeah."

"In Yarrow Point?"

Intensity, in both of them, mounted. "Yes."

Parker sucked in a deep breath. Frenetic intensity swirled around him.

Drew's color rose. "Why are you looking at me like that?"

"I...ah..." Parker's lips worked. "Your father saved my life." A rasp. "When I was a boy. He fought his way into our house and pulled me from the fire."

A gasp rounded the table. Drew paled. He dropped into his seat with a thud. "No shit?"

"No shit." Parker's laugh was harsh, but soul deep. "I never got to thank him."

The expression on Drew's face was amusing. He was so clearly torn. He wanted to hate Parker, but the firefighter, and the Boone, in him would not allow it.

"Well," he said gruffly. "I'm sure he'd be happy to meet you. Sometime."

"I would appreciate that. What he did...what you do... I can't imagine it."

Drew studied him for a moment, his focus zeroing in on the burn scar visible just above the collar of Parker's long-sleeved tee shirt. "So...you were in a fire?"

"Mmm hmm."

"What caused it?"

Parker stilled. "It was...arson."

"Oooh!" Drew perked up. "Arson." He loved arson.

Kaitlin relaxed. She knew—*knew*—everything would be okay. Now that Parker and Drew had something in common, they would become fast friends. Or at least not pummel each other very often.

Everyone else stifled a sigh. Because they knew. Once Drew started talking fires, there would be no other conversations for a long, long while.

Which was just fine with Kaitlin. She linked her fingers with Parker's and held his hand as he and Drew got acquainted.

CHAPTER THIRTEEN

They talked. They talked and talked.

And as fascinating as everyone found the conversation—or at least, Drew found it fascinating—something else bubbled in Parker's brain.

Kaitlin's fingers, twined in his, lit a fire in his belly. Reminded him, it had been far too long since he'd kissed her properly. Far too long since they'd been together. He shot her a look. Quirked a brow.

Her smile twitched. A minute twitch, but he caught it.

"Would you like to..." He glanced around the table, taking in the watching eyes. "Um... Go for a walk?"

"Oh yes," she said. "I would love some...fresh air."

Silence fell around the table.

"But I was just going to tell you about drafting," Drew sputtered.

Kaitlin nodded. "I think I'd really to go for a walk."

"You just got back from a walk—"

"It's such a beautiful day."

"But drafting is really cool. It's a system where we can draw water from, say, the ocean, to fight fires in places that don't have any hydrants— Hey! Where are you going?" he cried as Kaitlin and Parker stood.

"We'll be back. You can tell us then."

"But..."Drew leaped to his feet.

Holt took hold of his shirt and yanked him back down. "Tell *us*. I am enthralled."

"But…"

"Don't be gone long," Patrick warned. And it was a warning. "We're all going to Darby's later for dinner. I expect to see you there."

Kaitlin blew out a sigh, but nodded. "Okay, dad," she muttered and Parker chuckled.

Because, yeah, he'd been thinking the same thing. And also, he was going to get her on her own. *Finally.*

The walk over to Ash's house didn't take long at all, because they almost ran. He grabbed her once they were inside the door and tugged her against him and kissed her. "God, Kaitlin," he growled when they came up for air. "I've been needing this."

She yanked on his ears—he loved when she did that. "Me too."

Her mouth met his and she consumed him with a fervor that matched his own. His passion rose. With a groan, he pressed her against the wall and cupped her breast. She shivered, arched into his caress.

"Parker." A whisper.

"This way." Without disentangling, he walked her the short way down the hall to the one room on the ground floor. Relief flooded him; thank God he'd dropped his stuff in that room. He didn't think he could make it upstairs. Or downstairs. Or anywhere but here. And the condoms were in his suitcase.

Still kissing her, he sat her on the bed and undid her blouse. Once it was open, he took her breasts into his hands. Her nipples, hard points, burned into his palms. The breath locked in his lungs. "Kaitlin." He fumbled with the hook of her bra. She pushed him away and did it herself, ripping off her shirt at the same time. When she stood to remove her jeans, he dove for his suitcase, and pulled out a handful of condoms and dropped them on the bedside table, before kicking off his own jeans and tugging down his briefs. His shirt, he left on, as he always did. And then he joined her on the bed, walking toward her on his knees.

She smiled at him, a glorious invitation, and invocation, and his heart swelled.

God, she was beautiful.

His cock, already plenty swollen, thank you very much, throbbed.

He threaded his fingers through her hair and held her still as he kissed her again. "Baby, I've missed this."

"Me too." She ran her hands over his chest, his shoulders, his arms, his hips. They skimmed down over his thighs. To his astonishment, she grabbed his butt. Unbidden, a laugh escaped.

"You're pretty anxious," he teased.

"I am. It's been almost three days."

Three days. Far too long.

He tipped her back onto the pillows and settled over her, devouring her in an impassioned frenzy, nibbling at her cheek, her neck, her earlobe. She tasted wonderful. She smelled glorious.

"Hurry," she muttered, reaching for his cock and guiding him between her legs.

"You're not ready," he protested. "Besides, I want to taste you."

"Later," she said, squeezing him. "Taste me later. Right now I want you in."

A blazing cloud engulfed his sanity. Fortunately, there was a smidgen of sanity left, or he might have plowed into her, right then and there. "*I'm* not ready."

"You're ready." She licked her lips as she stroked his aching length.

He laughed and pulled away, but only to reach for one of the condoms. He'd made a vow to himself to always use one and he'd never broken it. And he never would. He ripped it open and yanked it on.

She wiggled her hips. "Hurry."

"I'm hurrying," he told her and then growled in his throat as the condom ripped at the intensity of his zeal. "Shit." He whipped it off and tried again, this time being more careful.

"Hurry," she pouted.

He loved her pout, but he did hurry.

Excitement boiled within him. Excitement and anticipation and perhaps a touch of panic. Need rode him hard.

Still, when he settled down beside her, he took a moment to stroke her, to check. To make sure she was—

Fuck.

She was ready. Ready and wet and...hot.

He groaned when he eased his fingers inside and she bathed them. "God, Kaitlin."

"Please," she murmured, staring up at him with those doe-like eyes wide, and limned with tears. "Do it. Make love to me now. I need you."

He couldn't not.

Easing over her, he spread her legs even more with his knees, and pressed in. She closed around him. Shivers raked his skin. He shuddered. "Oh, baby."

"Yes," she groaned.

He felt the rumble to his balls.

"I'll try to go slow..." he said. "But I have a powerful need."

She wrapped her arms around his neck and pulled him down. "I have a powerful need too, Parker," she whispered. "I need you to...fuck me. Hard."

Fuck. That word, from her lips, undid him.

He went wild. He fucked her. Hard.

She wailed at the first thrust, arching up into him and clenching him in an excruciating grip. He sucked in a breath and withdrew quickly, slamming into her again.

"Yes. Yes." She looped her legs around his and used him as leverage, lunging up even as he took her again and again.

He wasn't going to last. But then, neither was she. He could already see the signs of her coming orgasm. Her parted lips, the glazed look in her eyes, the huffing breaths. The increased frenzy of her lurching hips.

Heat coiled at the base of his balls sending delirious shards up into his belly. His cock tightened. His balls shrank to little nuts. It was coming. He was coming. It was...

She seized.

Threw back her head and opened her mouth and cried out, though it was without sound. Her body dissolved from a taut, hard tension, to a series of agonizing ripples and quakes.

Her manic clasp did him in. Delight and agony warred within him as he exploded, imploded, released in a flood of hot and blinding joy.

A great, delicious haze engulfed him. His heart thudded in his chest. His breath came out in ragged pants. He trembled as tremor after tremor walked through him.

Bliss.

Absolute and complete.

The tendrils of pleasure still clung as he eased out and moved to her side, then pulled her into his arms and kissed her. Her mouth was slack, her body, limp. They recovered together, gazing into each other's eyes.

"Parker?" She sighed.

"Yes, Kaitlin?"

"I love you."

His heart froze.

Nothing had prepared him for this. For this new rising bliss. This raging sear of gratitude. The sense of belonging. A potent…terror. All far too new to him. Too raw.

Nothing prepared him at all.

Other than staring at her, he didn't respond, but Kaitlin didn't mind. She didn't expect him to respond and she didn't require it.

She'd needed to say it.

And she felt better for it.

They were words she'd never said before, for an emotion she'd never experienced. And somehow, letting the words pass her lips, liberated her. She grinned at him and sprang from the bed, collecting her clothes. "We should probably get ready to go."

"Go?" He gaped at her as though in a daze.

She smacked him with her bra. "Dinner? At Darby's? Everyone will be waiting."

He flinched. "I completely forgot."

"Understandable," she said, tugging on her bra, her shirt and her jeans. "You were a little distracted, after all."

It was a relief to see him smile. See his colors lighten.

It had been a risk, sharing her feelings with him. It filled her heart with elation that she did not sense a withdrawal as a result of it. That would have been devastating.

After they dressed, they linked hands and made their way into town along the little path in the woods. Kaitlin loved this time of day, especially in the summer. The sun hung low in the sky and hit the earth at an angle, sending dazzling shafts through the canopy. The air was cool and the scent of pines and loam swirled around them.

"Beautiful," she whispered, gazing up through the lacy leaves.

"Yes," he said. And then he tugged her into his arms and kissed her.

It wasn't a declaration. But in a way, it was.

Happiness cascaded through her in delicious rivulets.

"We should go," she murmured against his lips.

He lifted his head. "Kaitlin?"

"Yes, Parker?"

"About what you said..."

She cupped his cheek. Thumbed the dent on his chin. "You don't have to say anything."

"I know. But I just want you to understand—"

"I do."

"You can't."

"I do understand."

His brow wrinkled. "Kaitlin—"

"Well *hoo-de-doo-dah*. Is this what the kids are calling *walks* nowadays?" Drew's voice, a little sharp, cut through the moment. Kaitlin sprang from Parker's arms and whirled to see everyone coming down the path.

She didn't growl at them for their terrible timing, but just barely. "Well, hey there. We were just heading to the bar ourselves."

"Were you?" Drew's brows lowered.

Kaitlin frowned at him. And then, deliberately, she smiled at everyone else, hooked her arm in Parker's and together, they resumed the walk to the bar, chatting and laughing. Though she noticed Drew whacked at a couple of ferns as he passed.

Darby's was busy on a summer evening, so they had to wait for a table for eight, but not long. Charmaine pulled three tables together, wiped them down and handed them their menus with a smile.

"I don't know why she doesn't just bring us our food," Cam grunted. "We always get the same thing."

Kristi chuckled. "Maybe we should all order something completely different...just to throw her off."

"That would be cruel," Bella said with a grin. "We totally should. Charmaine brought them all water and—without asking—a pitcher of beer and a tray full of glasses.

Holt shot her a devastating grin. It seemed to stall her mid-movement. "You must have read my mind, darling," he purred.

Drew barked a laugh. "She doesn't have to be psychic to know we like beer. We come here every weekend."

"Not every weekend."

"Practically every weekend."

"Right." Charmaine wiped her hands on her Darby's Darlings apron and flipped open a pad. "Are you ready to order?"

Drew tipped his head to the side. "Don't you *know* what we want?"

Her smile was cheeky. She went around the table pointing at each one of them in turn, saying, "Double bacon cheeseburger with fries, Double bacon cheeseburger with onion rings, steak medium well no fries, vegan patty, fish and chips, cobb salad with extra avocado and…" She stalled when she came to Parker. "Burger and fries?"

Laughter rounded the table.

"Damn, she is psychic," Drew crowed.

Charmaine winked at him. "I'll be right back with your shot of Jack." And then she flounced away, leaving Drew with his mouth agape.

"How did she know I wanted a shot of Jack?" he sputtered.

Patrick chuckled. "I guess she really is psychic."

"Or she's been doing this a long time?" Kristi filled her glass with water and took a sip. "I swear, that woman works harder than anyone I know."

"We only come on the weekends," Cam said. "It's probably not so crazy during the week."

"Still… How cool would it to be a psychic waitress?" Something in Drew's tone caught Kaitlin's attention; it sent pings down her spine. He glanced at her, then at Parker. His jaw firmed. His intention rolled over her in a wave. *Oh no.* "What do you think, Kaitlin?"

She steeled her spine, forcing her panic away. "I wouldn't know, Drew," she said. "I'm not a waitress."

"But you are a psychic."

Parker stiffened at her side. Kaitlin tried not to wince at the sudden shift in his energy. "I'm not a mind reader, Drew."

"Aren't you?" Drew's laugh was harsh. His gaze raked around the table. "Isn't she?"

"Drew." Patrick's voice rumbled a dark warning.

"What? We all know it. You know it, don't you, Parker? You're her... *boyfriend*. Surely you would know that."

She could feel Parker staring at her. Sense his confusion and a ripple of fear and betrayal. Kaitlin fiddled with the paper of her straw. She couldn't bear to look at him. Couldn't bear to see her worst fears come true.

Oh damn.

Damn Drew.

Damn herself.

She should have been brave. She should have just taken the bull by the horns and told him.

"Kaitlin?" Parker's voice was low, almost a whisper. "Kaitlin, look at me."

It took everything in her to tip her head, to meet his eyes.

And yes. Everything she'd felt was there in his expression. "Parker—"

He glanced around the table, then took her arm and tugged. "Let's go for a walk."

"Really?" Did Drew need to bellow? "Another walk? What is it with you two and walking—"

"Drew." Patrick again, in tandem with Holt. "Shut up."

Kaitlin ignored the sudden tension at the table and slipped from her seat, following Parker like a zombie. She knew. She just knew what was coming, and it devastated her.

He led her out the front door and waved to the bench under the overhang of the bar's porch where the smokers usually hung out. They were not there tonight. "Can we talk?" he asked.

"Sure." He might not have heard her, as her chin was tucked so low. But she sat, and he sat next to her. Silence wreathed them. It was not a comfortable silence. She couldn't stand it. She had to say something. "I'm sorry I didn't tell you sooner."

"Tell me?"

"About it."

He tipped her face up. "Tell me now."

Oh lord. He wanted her to tell him about it. He wanted to know what it was. She comforted herself with the knowledge he hadn't just backed away, the way some people did.

"I don't know how." She shrugged. "It's just who I am, Parker."

"You said you don't read minds…"

She snorted. "No. It's colors and feelings. Energy patterns. Things like that." She set her hand on his arm. "Are you freaked out?"

His smile was a miracle. "A little."

"Why?"

He shrugged. "Everyone likes to think they have secrets."

"I don't know everything."

"That's a relief."

"Just most things. And with some people, only when I touch them. That's why…"

"Why, what?"

"That's why I hadn't, you know, before now."

"You know?"

"You know."

"Well, I don't know." He gusted a laugh, but it was a shallow one. "I'm *not* psychic."

She became suddenly obsessed with the hem of her blouse. "Why I'd never…been with someone."

He gaped at her. His throat worked. "Wait. What?"

"It was always painful, when I touched someone. Always…too much. But when I touched you, there was that one flash of pain…and then nothing but pleasure. It—"

"Wait… You'd never *been* with someone before?"

She stared up at him, her eyes wide. Shook her head. "Just you." A whisper.

His jaw went slack. He was quiet for quite some time. "Well, shit, Kaitlin. You should have told me."

"Why?"

"So I could, I don't know, make it better? Be gentle?"

"You were wonderful. You are wonderful."

He shook his head. "I just can't wrap my brain around this."

Her heart sank. She set her hand on his arm. "I'm only a little psychic." Okay. A lie. Probably.

His snort surprised her. "Not *that*, Kaitlin. Christ, you were a virgin?"

"Yes."

"How could I not have known that?"

"Did you expect a fanfare? Confetti fluttering from the ceiling?" She bit back a smile. Confetti would have been nice.

"Isn't there supposed to be pain or blood or something awful?"

"Silly, this isn't the middle ages. And I had no pain. It was different—"

"Different?" He reared back, an affronted expression on his face.

"But pleasant. Very pleasant."

"Different, how?"

"Parker, it was wonderful. Just weird to feel so…full." She stroked his arm. "You are quite large."

A flush rose on his cheeks. "Well," he said gruffly.

"I enjoyed it very much."

"Well, I… You did?"

"I did. It was very nice."

"Nice?" he roared.

"*Very* nice. Can we stop talking about this?"

He frowned at her. "Nice?"

"Very."

"Humph."

They sat in silence for a moment and Kaitlin tried to read him. There was still some confusion and fear twining around him, but there was acceptance as well.

"Do you mind very much that I have this gift?"

His forehead wrinkled. "Mind?"

"Some people…" She dropped her head. "Well some people are afraid of me. Some people hate it."

He cupped her cheeks and forced her to look at him. "I'm not afraid of you. Kaitlin. If this is part of what makes you who you are, how could I hate it?"

Something inside her, something that had been tightly held for far too long, released. Joy coursed through her. "Thank you, Parker." She kissed him. "Thank you for understanding. It means everything to me." It meant the world.

"Sure." He tucked his arm around her and pulled her close. "Just be patient with me while I work this all out, okay?"

She nestled closer. "Okay."

Kristi poked her head out the door. "Hey, you guys," she said. "Our food's here."

"Thanks." Kaitlin waved and Kristi went back inside. "Shall we?" she asked.

"Okay." He stood and reached out a hand to her. His palm was warm against hers. They started back inside when suddenly he stilled. "Do you see…dead people?" he asked.

Something in his tone snagged her attention. She snorted a laugh. "No."

He collapsed in mock relief.

"But I know people…."

He gaped at her."Seriously?"

"Yes. Is there anyone you wanted to reach?"

She shouldn't have asked. His energy shifted sharply, his muscles bunched. But then, after a moment, he relaxed. "My mother, maybe." He kissed her forehead. "Maybe, someday."

He looped his arm around her and she threaded her fingers through his at her shoulder. "When you're ready, just ask."

They stepped inside the darkened bar and Kaitlin blew out a sigh of relief. She should have told him, but she hadn't. Now he knew, and he hadn't run away. There was something quite gratifying in that fact. That and the simmering sense that he was, indeed, the one.

Also gratifying was Drew's pout when he saw them entwined and realized his little outing hadn't had the effect he'd hoped.

She shot him an evil grin.

He choked on his French fry.

Served him right.

CHAPTER FOURTEEN

After dinner with Kaitlin's friends, which was more pleasant than he expected, they all headed home, although Drew stayed behind to play some pool and, Parker suspected, flirt with the waitress. When they reached the turn for Ash's driveway, Parker glanced at Kaitlin.

He didn't say it. Didn't say, *are you coming in?* But she seemed to read his meaning because she smiled and waved her friends on.

Of course she read his meaning. She was *psychic*.

It should have freaked him out, this little tidbit. He'd spent most of his life hiding huge chunks of himself from the world. The thought of everything being revealed, everything exposed to her, should have terrified him. It did not.

In fact, it was almost a relief. He didn't have to hide anything from Kaitlin. He couldn't if he wanted to.

It was as though she, and she alone, understood him. Saw him for who he was. And he liked the way he looked in her eyes.

The house was dark when they entered, so he flicked on the lights. "Do you want anything?" he asked, because he couldn't think of anything else to say.

"Just you."

A shiver rippled through him. The light in her eye invigorated him. "Just me?" He pulled her into his arms, there in the hall, and kissed her. "I'm yours. Do with me what you will." It was a joke.

And not.

She chuckled and wiggled closer, rubbing her belly against his cock. Heat rose. Lust rose. And something more than that.

He wanted this woman, needed her maybe, with a passion that was probably unwise.

But unwise or not, he couldn't find it in him to resist.

Thank God the bedroom wasn't far away.

Parker was gentle as he backed her into the bedroom until her legs hit the bed. There was a tenor to his kiss she had not experienced before—a softness, a vulnerability—but she liked it. His fingers trembled as he unbuttoned her blouse, taking him longer than it should have, but when she tried to intervene, he pushed her hand away and murmured, "Let me."

Her blouse fell from her shoulders and he caressed her exposed skin, running his palm over her in an enthralling, drugging pattern. He stroked her for some time, invigorating her skin, waking her, making her feel alive and cherished. His knuckles scraped over her nipples and she gasped. Their gazes met. His lips tweaked up in a crooked smile, but he didn't remove her bra. Instead, he turned her around, so she faced the bed, and proceeded to give her back the same delicious treatment.

It was a new experience for Kaitlin, this intensity of touching—his palms, warm on her skin, drawing delight on her.

There was no pain. No cacophony. No anxiety. Only bliss.

He kissed her neck, the cap of her shoulder, then trailed his mouth down her spine, tasting her.

"Parker…" She whirled around to find him on his knees. He stared up at her with a smile and reached for the snap of her jeans. Slowly, he slid the zipper down and eased them off, again, leaving her underwear on.

The look in his eyes made her knees buckle. She clutched his shoulder to steady herself. "Kaitlin, you are so lovely," he said, leaning in to kiss her belly. His hands roved. Over her lower back, down her thighs to the backs of her knees, and down to her feet. He made long strokes that sent ripples dancing along her nerves. "I want to worship you."

"W-worship me?"

In response, he hooked his thumbs in her panties and nudged

them down. It was a leisurely journey, with his mouth tracking their passage. When he reached her ankles, she lifted one foot, and then the other, and stepped out of her underwear. He kissed his way back up, still rubbing her, warming her…but he stopped when he reached the crux of her thighs and stroked her curls.

She sucked in a breath.

He leaned forward. Opened her and touched his tongue to her thrumming button.

Kaitlin seized. Pleasure and passion rained through her. A groan escaped from her throat. He circled her, lightly lapping and licking at the aching nerves. He continued to stroke her with his palms, while with his mouth, he incited her to greater passion.

When he sucked her in, nibbled, she lost her balance and fell onto the bed. He followed her, relentlessly, consuming her with a rising fervor. His moans and murmurs sent shocks of vibration through her body, shot her through with spirals of delight. He pleasured her until everything tightened. Her nipples, her belly, the muscles in her legs.

An ache began, deep within her, a gnawing hunger, a raging desire…for more.

"Parker…"

Without halting his agonizing exploration, he slipped two fingers inside her, stroking, searching. He found some arcane spot, some bundle of sensitive nerves, and he touched her.

Everything within her constricted, until the tension was unbearable and raw and delicious. Her lungs seized. Heat rose from her belly to her neck in a scorching tide. The entirety of her world, her universe, narrowed down to the point where Parker's mouth suckled her, his fingers nudged. Her body shook. Her soul contracted.

He thrust deeper, sucked harder and—

The tremble began in her belly and swept out in ever-increasing arcs. She shuddered, quaked, howled as a delicious sensation, one she had only known with him, flooded her. Her vision went cloudy, then burst into a rain of bright and sparkling lights as a glorious bliss descended.

As she recovered, he crawled up beside her on the bed, still trailing his palms over her belly, her hips, her breasts.

He was careful, though, to avoid her nipples. They were hard points and they ached for his touch. She pouted at him. He grinned.

"Did you enjoy that, my darling?"

"Yes, Parker. But don't you want to take off my bra?"

He stilled. His intensity bore into her. "I would like to…take something else off first."

Her joking mood faded. She could tell from his expression, from his somber energy, this was no joking matter. This was serious. Deadly serious.

"W-what would you like to take off?"

His throat worked. "My shirt."

Her heart slowed, and then launched into a manic rhythm. "Okay."

"You won't run away?"

"No. You didn't run…when you found out about me."

"You're not hideous."

She smiled and stroked his face, thumbing the dent in his cheek. "Neither are you."

He sucked in a deep breath and took the hem of his shirt in his hands…and peeled it off.

She stared at him, taking it all in. The angry scars, the tired ones, the puckered circle where a bullet had pierced him. He bore her scrutiny courageously, stalwartly, showing her the kind of man he truly was. Brave. Beautiful.

But then, she'd known all along.

"Oh Parker," she sighed. "I wish you could see yourself the way I see you." She came up on her knees and put her palms on his shoulders and she did for him what he had done for her. She touched him. Stroked him. Loved every inch of him.

His lashes fluttered, his lips parted. A groan, some dark and deep release, rumbled from his chest.

He took her in his arms and laid her down on the bed, removing her bra and releasing her breasts into his keeping. He kissed them and nuzzled them and brought her, again, to a frenzy. And then, never dropping her gaze, he settled between her legs and entered her.

It was so much more than it had been before—any of the other times. Because this was Parker, bare before her, and she was bare before him. And still, they loved each other.

He'd never said it, but she'd *heard* it.

He began slowly, reverently, filling her in one relentless, deliberate stroke after another. But then, when she began to wriggle beneath him, to demand more, he increased his pace. The feel of his cock sluicing in and out of her body was exquisite. Each stroke scraped against delighted nerves, stretching her, filling her. Soon, Kaitlin was mindless again. Crazed with passion. The wet sounds of their loving echoed through the room.

"Parker, yes," she cried, sinking her fingers into his hair and tugging at him. Urging him on.

"Ah," he groaned as he slammed into her again. "Yes. Yes. Yes." Each cry in tandem with a frenzied thrust. His cock swelled inside her. His movements became faster still, and his passion tipped her over the edge. As she closed on him, he sucked in a breath and his body seized.

Heat filled her, flooded her, sending her into another, a new, paroxysm of delight.

Chest heaving, he dropped his head on her shoulder and gasped for breath. She held him, soothed him, running her hands over his back, his neck, his buttocks, soaking in his essence and blanketing him in serene cloud.

He lifted his head and stared into her eyes. "Are you...okay?"

She smiled. Touched his cheek. "Very okay. Are you okay?"

"God, Kaitlin." His throat worked. "I..."

"I know, Parker." Simply that. *I know*. She did.

He rolled to the side, taking her with him, loving the exhilarating feel of her skin against his. Chest to chest, groin to groin. Funny how something so simple could become so important when a man was denied it for so long. A human touch. A caress...without a recoil. It was priceless.

She was priceless.

He never wanted to let her go.

Ever.

She shifted and his cock slipped out. He reached for the condom and froze.

Shit.

"Parker? What is it?"

Shit.

He released a groan; it sounded a little like a wail to his ears. "Damn it, Kaitlin, I forgot to use a condom."

"A…condom?"

"I'm sorry. I always do. Always." It mortified him to ask, but he had to. "You're on birth control, right?"

Her expression blanked. Horror skirled in his belly.

"You are on birth control. Right?"

A tiny shake of those red curls sent dread skittering along his veins.

Shit. Shit. Shit.

"There was never any need…"

Right. Because she was a freaking *virgin.*

Releasing her, he collapsed on the pillows and scrubbed his face. What a disaster. What a travesty. He'd been so careful for so long, only to have this woman waltz into his life and steal his heart and make him *feel* and forget everything—

Her palm on his chest scuttled his thoughts. Completely interrupted his self-flagellation.

"Parker." And, when he didn't respond, "Parker." She pried his hands from his face. "It's going to be okay. Relax."

"I can't relax, Kaitlin. You just don't understand."

She sent him a sardonic look. "Don't I?"

How could she? Psychic or not, how could she understand? How could anyone?

"So tell me."

"I made a vow. A vow, Kaitlin." A sacred vow he knew he could never break.

"A vow to always wear a condom?" It was annoying the way her lips tweaked, as though she found this amusing. *This.* The greatest disaster of his life. And he'd had some pretty big disasters.

"A vow to never have children." Pain and regret flooded him in an unexpected wave. A little girl with bouncing red curls and impish green eyes? Or a brave boy he could protect and teach how to be a good man? "I'll never have children."

She stroked his chest. "Never?"

He kissed her forehead. "I can't. I just…can't. What if it turns out I'm like him?"

Her smile warmed him, but did not chase away the shadows. "You're not your father."

"I could be." He bunched his fists. "I could be like him. If I let it out."

"It?"

"The passion. The emotion." He was scared to death one day he would wake up and see his father's face in the mirror.

Kaitlin's expression went fierce, which was adorable on her. "You're not like him."

"How can you know that?"

She grinned. "First of all, I'm psychic."

He snorted a laugh.

"If there was anything truly dark in your soul, I would know. I would see it. I sure as heck wouldn't be here now. But it goes far beyond that."

"What-what do you mean?"

"Remember what Patrick said? About judging a man by his actions?"

"Yes." It was a good standard. Sometimes the only standard.

"Even if I couldn't *see* what a good, gentle, loving man you are—a true pure soul... Even if I didn't see that in your aura, I would know."

He wanted to believe her.

Oh, God, he would give anything for her to be...right.

"How would you know?"

She wrapped her arms around him, as though preparing for a rough ride. She turned her head away, so he couldn't see her face. He suspected she needed to, so he didn't turn it back.

When she began, her voice was low. He had to struggle to hear. "There was a night in college. A long time ago. A party. Wild. Crazy. Loud. You wandered upstairs—probably to get away from the noise—and discovered a bunch of your frat buddies had a girl trapped in a room. A silly girl. A stupid girl who'd gone to the party because it sounded fun. She didn't expect that their kind of fun was very different from hers.

"Those boys took the girl to a remote room in the house and wouldn't let her leave. They were going to...r-rape her." Her voice broke. "But you made them stop. You didn't hit them or threaten them. You just said 'Leave her alone.' Do you remember that?"

He shook his head, then stilled as a memory enveloped him. It was blurry—he'd been drinking then—but he remembered. A slender girl with brown hair, her fragile chin trembling, her wide doe eyes, frightened. He'd seen that look before—on his mother's face—and it had infuriated him to see it again. His gaze flicked to Kaitlin's. "I do. I do remember."

"A violent man would have fought them. A bastard would have let them keep going. But you saved that girl."

He pulled her closer. "You really are psychic, aren't you?"

She drew in a breath and peeped up at him, her fragile chin trembling, her wide doe eyes filled with tears. "I was that girl, Parker. I'm the one you saved."

"But…" He stroked her hair.

"Mmm." She nestled closer. "I was a brunette then." She cracked a grin. "It was during my rebellious phase." Her palm skimmed his cheek. "Thank you," she whispered, pulling him down for a kiss. "You saved me. You are my hero, for now and forever."

Her words warmed him, renewed him, thawed something deep inside that had long been encased in ice.

He was someone's hero.

Holy God.

"You'll be a wonderful father one day, Parker, if it ever happens. You will be magnificent at it. I know it."

He allowed himself to relax, to sink into the possibility. Long-held fears and worries and regrets slipped away, evaporated before the force of her conviction. It was miraculous, having someone who believed in you. It changed a man, deep, inside where no one could see the scars.

"Thank you, Kaitlin." He kissed her.

"Thank you, Parker. You're the one who saved me."

No. She'd saved him.

CHAPTER FIFTEEN

They spent the rest of the night and most of the next morning in bed, making love and talking and soaking in each other's presence. Parker didn't want the weekend to end, but he knew it would.

He sat with Kaitlin and her friends on the ferry on the way home and enjoyed the easy camaraderie, laughter and jokes. He also enjoyed their acceptance. Even Drew seemed to be warming to him. A little.

Mostly, he enjoyed sitting on the hard banquette by the window with his arm around Kaitlin, staring out at the water as the ferry sliced through the Sound. An eagle soared overhead and he caught her eye. They shared a smile.

When the Seattle skyline came into view, she dragged him out on the cold deck, in the whipping wind and the spattering rain, so they could watch it loom closer. It was a beautiful skyline. A beautiful city. Even under dark clouds. Perhaps because of them.

He wrapped his arm around her and they stood and watched until the warning horn blared and a garbled message came over the loudspeakers urging them back to their vehicles. He walked her to the lower deck and kissed her before helping her into her car.

The ferry landed with a lurch. Engines started up all around him.

He leaned in through her window and kissed her again. "I gotta go," he said.

She smiled. "See you tonight?"

"Of course." They had plans for dinner. Chinese again. He was going to teach her how to use chopsticks if it was the last thing he did. With a smile, he left her.

The week that followed was a blur. During the day he dealt with briefs and meetings and the occasional irate call from Tucker. But at night, it was all Kaitlin.

That he loved her, insanely and passionately, was never in doubt. She'd said the words to him, and now he wanted, rather desperately, to say them to her. But he didn't know how. It needed to be something spectacular. A declaration she would never forget. He worked through scenario after scenario in his head, but all that did was make him antsy. He'd never told anyone he loved them before—not since he was five. He wasn't sure how it was done. And it scared him as well.

On Thursday he got a call from Kaitlin, asking him to meet her client at a bookstore south of the city, in Tukwila. It was an odd place to meet, but Parker understood the need to be clandestine. This woman, the client, didn't want to expose herself in a place she might be seen by someone who knew her, or her husband.

So he drove to Tukwila.

It was a new age bookstore, filled with self-help CDs and crystals and essential oils. The trails of incense hung heavy on the air. He made his way to the back where the proprietors had set up a rustic coffee shop. His mood lifted when he saw Kaitlin.

She stood as he approached. Her body was tense, her features tight. It was so unlike her, it caught his attention. He kissed her. "Is everything all right?"

"Oh yes," she huffed. "Of course. I… We… This is nerve wracking for her." She gestured to the woman sitting hunched at their table, facing the wall. Her hair was an unnatural brassy blonde and tumbled over her shoulders in a contrived fall. Parker suspected it was a wig. "Come and meet her." Kaitlin tugged him over and waved at the open seat.

"Susan, this is the man I was telling you about. Parker. Parker, this is Susan."

The woman reached out a slender hand, which trembled as she looked up at him. His gut tightened. Yellow bruises covered her face, along with cuts and scars. But it was the expression in her eyes that devastated him. He'd see that expression before. Frightened.

Defeated. He'd seen it many times.

In his mother's eyes.

"Susan." He took her hand. Gently. "Nice to meet you. Kaitlin tells me you could use a lawyer."

She nodded. "Yes. Thank you-thank you for coming."

"My pleasure." It was. For once, he could do something with his knowledge. Something that mattered. Something that could make a difference. For one woman, one child at least.

He pulled a folder out of his briefcase and a pen from his suit pocket and tried to make his tone as matter-of-fact and comforting as he could. "Shall we start with the basics?"

She nodded.

"Okay. Great. What's your name?" He poised the pen to write.

"Susan Talbot."

He nodded and scratched that in the first box of his intake form. But then his pen stilled.

"But my married name is Tucker."

His heart thudded, hard. His throat constricted and a nauseating snarl rose in his belly. "Susan Tucker?"

She nodded.

He glanced at Kaitlin, who sat quietly on the other side if the table, hands folded. "Susan Tucker?" She nodded as well.

"Parker...what is it?"

Panic roiled, remorse swamped him. Goddamn it. He'd really wanted to help this woman. She was so like his mother but— "I can't help. I have to leave." He pushed away from the table, collected his things and strode from the shop.

"What?" Kaitlin's cry followed him. *She* followed him. She caught him at the door. "Parker, what are you talking about?"

He raked his fingers through his hair. "Shit, Kaitlin. My firm is representing her husband." The brute. The guy who nearly killed her...and her daughter. *Fuck.* "I can't be her lawyer."

The expression on her face made him want to die. Sink into the ground. He'd disappointed her. Let her down. He felt, somehow, like less of a man. "I am so sorry, baby, but I can't do this."

"Parker, she needs you."

"I have some friends I can recommend." He fished for his wallet. For business cards. Something. A dark cloud dimmed his vision.

"Don't say anything more. Don't tell me where she's staying. Don't tell me anything." He found a card for a friend from another firm and shoved it into her hands. "I have to go, baby." He kissed her. Please God, let her forgive him for this. "I'm so sorry."

This time she let him go. He stormed to his car and threw his briefcase in the back and slumped into the driver's seat, covering his face. *Shit. Shit, shit, shit.* What were the odds that *she* would be Tucker's wife? And now that he'd seen, with his own eyes, what the bastard was capable of, how was he going to defend him?

Well, he couldn't. What Tucker had done was indefensible. Parker was going to have to recuse himself. Let Nate take the case. There was no way on God's green earth that he was going to represent Tucker.

It meant his promotion, of course. Probably a hit to his entire career. But he didn't care.

He didn't care.

Damn Tucker. Damn him to hell.

And all the men like him.

He felt ill by the time he made it back to the office. His stomach was churning and the pain had reappeared at the base of his head. His mind was in turmoil. The nasty traffic hadn't helped.

As he drove back from Tukwila, he realized Kaitlin's friend had been right. Lawyers were not very nice people. He ran through the greatest cases of his career, thought about the things he'd done and the things he'd hired people to do.

Nothing had mattered, but the win.

Nothing.

But now, a woman and her child stood at risk. People who had a lot to lose because of men like him.

And he hated it.

How many other lives had he ruined by being a phenomenal, dispassionate lawyer? How many?

His phone rang as he dropped into his plush chair in his plush office. He glared at it. He didn't want to talk to anyone.

But he had to. It was his job.

He sighed and picked up the receiver. "Rieth."

"Hey Parker," Gilley's voice wafted over the line.

"Hey buddy." Parker scrubbed at his temple. The pain had migrated there. "What's up?"

"Great news. I found her."

His heart lurched. "What? Who?"

"I found Susan Tucker. She didn't skip the country after all. She's been holed up in a women's shelter in downtown Seattle. One of my guys saw her getting into a car this afternoon and gave me a head's up."

Fuck.

She'd been spotted. Coming to see *him*. One thought burned through his brain. He had to warn her.

"Can you sit on it for a while?" He could lose his job, just for asking, but he didn't care.

Silence crackled over the line. "Well, I could have. But I thought there was a rush on this, so I already called Tucker."

Oh God. Something bitter tickled the back of Parker's throat. "You did?"

"Yeah. Bartsow gave the go-ahead. Pretty insistent about it too. Tucker has the address. He's heading over there now."

Parker's heart stopped. Pain filled his chest. He gasped for breath. Hell. Tucker was on his way over to the shelter. And Kaitlin was there. Panic raged through him.

"That's not a good idea, Gilley." He hated the warble in his voice. "Tell him that's not a good idea."

"Yeah, I told him. Have you tried telling him anything? He's convinced she'll escape again if he doesn't get her now."

Get her now.

Shit.

A vision flamed through him of a man, storming into a women's shelter, a shelter that had taken them in—he and his mother after one of his father's rampages. He'd 'gotten them.' Dragged them home.

A day later his mother was dead.

"Give me the address." He scribbled it down and glanced at his watch. How much time did he have? Could he get there before Tucker? "Where was he coming from?"

"How the hell should I know?"

"Yeah. Right. Thanks Gilley."

"And Parker—"

Parker disconnected the call. He should never have hired Gilley. He was too damn good. But he hadn't known. Hadn't realized.

Madly, he scrambled for his cell and punched in Kaitlin's number.

"Hello Parker." Her voice was soft, sweet, lyrical. She had no idea. No idea what was coming.

"Kaitlin, where are you?"

"We just got back."

"Are you at the shelter?"

"Yes. What—"

"Get them out of there, now."

"What?"

"Get Susan and Lily out of there. Tucker knows where they are. He's on his way."

"Oh no—"

The line went dead. Parker could only hope he'd given her enough notice. Only hope that she could spirit Susan and Lily away before Tucker barged into the shelter. Regardless, he had to leave. Leave now. Go to her. He couldn't bear the thought of Kaitlin facing that brutal man all on her own—

"What the hell do you think you're doing?" An infuriated voice snarled through his office. Parker looked up to see Barstow in the doorway, hands on his hips. "Did you just tip off Tucker's wife?" Incredulity wafted from him.

Parker stood and collected his things. "Yes," he said, as he rushed past.

"Rieth!" The bellow stopped him in his tracks. His boss stared at him with a piercing glare. "You are not the man I thought you were."

Parker fought back the manic urge to laugh. "No sir, I guess I'm not."

In a rush, Kaitlin bundled Susan and Lily into her car and drove them to her house. There wasn't time to arrange something else and Susan's husband would never track her here.

Her heart was filled with gratitude toward Parker for the warning. He hadn't needed to call. In fact, she worried that he might get in trouble at work for tipping off the client's quarry. But a woman's life was worth more than a stupid paycheck. She loved that he recognized that.

Glancing over her shoulder, she hurried Susan and Lily through the back door of her house. She didn't know why she was so nervous. Probably the adrenaline pumping in her system. Her life was calm, uneventful, filled with peace and healing. She wasn't used to drama. She'd certainly never run away from a threat.

Her paranoia was irrational. No one could know where they were. But she pulled down the shades, just in case. She didn't feel safe until she threw the bolt on the front door. And even then, her pulse hammered in her throat.

"Would you like something to eat? Chocolate, perhaps?" she asked as she opened the cupboards and pulled out a large bar. Her craving was strong. Susan glanced at the bar and then looked at Kaitlin quizzically. "It helps," she explained. "I have soup too."

"Soup would be fine." Susan moved into the kitchen and nudged Kaitlin out of the way. "Let me cook."

They had clam chowder and crackers and watched as Lily played with Boomer and Brandy on the floor. It was delightful seeing the little girl laugh and romp with the kittens. Eventually Kaitlin's heartbeat slowed.

"Well," Susan gusted, taking a sip of the hot chocolate Kaitlin had made. It was creamy and comforting and restorative. At least to Kaitlin. She'd also eaten an entire bar of chocolate, though she had shared some with Lily. "This has been an eventful day."

Kaitlin smiled at her. She'd come to really like the woman. She was so brave and courageous in the face of monumental troubles. Kaitlin hoped she would be as strong if she ever had to face adversity. Not only was Susan dealing with a divorce from a very unpleasant man, she was facing poverty and homelessness. But still, she kept her chin up.

"It has been. But everything is okay now." It didn't feel okay—Kaitlin still had that tingle of dread coursing through her—but she felt the lie was forgivable. And it paid off, because Susan laughed. It was the first time Kaitlin had seen her relax enough to do so. She had a lovely laugh. "Tomorrow we'll move you to one of the other shelters. Maybe one out of town. We have a couple up north."

"Away from the city?" Susan's eyes brightened. "I'd like that."

"And I have a couple friends I'd like you to meet." Lucy, for one. Emily. They'd both done lots of work at the shelter and believed in what they were doing there. And they had resources. Maybe they could help Susan find a job. "We'll work it out. I'm…sorry about Parker."

A shadow crossed Susan's expression. "That's okay."

"I had no idea his firm was representing your husband. But he gave me some other contacts."

Susan nodded. "I understand." She took another sip of her cocoa, a desperate sip, as though the chocolate could solve all her problems. Kaitlin could relate to the hope. She took a sip as well and then laughed as a pouf of whipped cream clung to her nose. Lily and Susan giggled as well.

They all watched as Boomer stalked Brandy around the legs of the coffee table, and then pounced. Lily shrieked with amusement as the two rolled, clenched together in a feline battle.

Kaitlin loved the way Lily's eyes danced. The way the darkness lifted. The way she seemed, once again, like a little girl delighted by the wonders of the world.

How wonderful it would be to have a child. A child to hold and adore and protect. She set her hand on her belly and thought of Parker. Parker's child. What would that be like? A great thrill welled in her chest.

He was—

A pounding at the door scuttled her thoughts. A roiling angst rushed in, filling her mind. Dread churned in her gut. She shot a look at Susan and Lily. They'd both gone preternaturally still.

"*Susan!*" A bitter snarl resonated through the flimsy barrier. Kaitlin's blood went cold. As cold as the fury in his voice.

"Oh God," Susan whispered.

"Hide," she hissed, pushing Susan and Lily through the kitchen and up the back stairs toward the bedroom.

"Where?"

"My bedroom. The closet. It has a false wall." Kaitlin rushed into the room and whipped open the closet door, and pulled off the false wall some previous owner had installed. Downstairs the pounding and yelling continued. It seemed as though the entire house shook.

Just as she closed the door on Susan and Lily's hunched and

trembling forms, a crash sounded downstairs. Kaitlin whirled and ran through the hall, then tore down the stairs. Her stained glass window lay smashed on the foyer floor, her beautiful purple flowers in shattered shards. A hand pushed through, feeling for the lock.

Oh lord!

She cast around for a weapon of some kind. A jacket on the hall tree… An umbrella… She ran into the kitchen and grabbed a knife. She didn't think she had the nerve to use it, but it was something.

He burst into the house as she returned to the hall, a huge, muscled man with a blunt nose and a snarl curling his entire face. "Where the fuck is my wife?" he bellowed.

Kaitlin attempted to calm her battering heart. She tipped up her chin. "I have no idea who you're talking about," she said.

"Bullshit." He swung out his fist in a rage and punched a hole in the drywall. Kaitlin stared at it. "My man followed you here from the shelter. All of you. Where is my wife?" He was big. Muscled. Furious.

"You-you must be mistaken. Please leave."

"The fuck." He punched the wall again and Kaitlin flinched. She held the knife before her like a shield. Somewhere in the mists of her mind, she wondered why she hadn't grabbed a larger one. "I want my wife, and I want her now." His low growl rumbled through her. She refused to be cowed. He stepped closer. She lifted the knife.

"Leave now. I'm calling the police."

"Fuck the police." It was a surprise when he hit her. No one had ever hit her before. That probably stunned her more than the blow itself. His fist was enormous and it caught her on the cheek. Shock washed through her along with a blazing pain as her neck snapped back. She reeled and fell against the table.

He followed her, stalking her like a beast. "Where is she?"

"I don't know who you're talking about."

"Goddamn it!" His eyes bulged. The veins on his neck stood out. His face was red and sheened with sweat. "Tell me!" He put his fingers around her throat and squeezed. Lights danced.

Please God, she prayed. *Let someone hear. Let someone come.*

But no one did.

She scratched at his hands. He tightened his hold and a wave of nausea swept through her.

She was aware of the room, the stillness of the air. The patter of

Boomer and Brandy's little feet as they ran from this threat. The scents of cocoa and clam chowder. The ticking of her clock. She fought for breath, but couldn't draw it in.

Her vision blurred. Her muscles went slack. She fell to the floor, a limp pile, barely aware of Tucker stepping over her and storming up the stairs, bellowing, "Susan! Susan! Where the fuck are you, bitch?"

And then, everything went black.

CHAPTER SIXTEEN

Parker's breath caught as he swerved to miss another car. After Gilley's call, giving him an update on Susan Tucker's location, he'd changed course and driven to Kaitlin's house like a mad man.

His heart had clenched when Gilley had given him the address. *Her* address. His mouth had filled with a bitter taste. Sweat prickled his brow. He had to get to her in time. He had to.

He'd broken the law as he veered wildly through traffic, something he swore he'd never do. But there was no time to pull over and call the police, so he dialed 9-1-1 and barked Kaitlin's address, even as he ran a red light.

He screeched to a halt before Kaitlin's house, leaped out and ran up the stairs. A snarl of horror curled through him when he saw the front door, wide open, the stained glass window, smashed. He hoped to hell he was on time.

Something deep inside, a dark voice, told him he was not.

He ran inside and looked around wildly.

A flash of red caught his attention.

His blood went cold.

He rounded the corner and saw her, lying on the floor. Still.

Kaitlin.

God. He couldn't...he couldn't... he couldn't live without her.

A scorching pain raged through him. He pushed it away and rushed to her side. "Kaitlin? Kaitlin, baby?"

Her lips were blue.

146

Fuck.

He felt for a pulse. It was there, but faint. But she wasn't breathing.

The fingerprints marring her skin made his vision blur as fury and fear warred within him.

Scrambling to remember first aid classes from God knows when, he put his hand on her forehead and tipped back her head. He pinched her nose and covered her mouth with his, breathing in gently.

Her chest rose, but other than that, there was no response.

Oh, where the hell was 9-1-1?

He breathed in again and again. Each puff more panicked than the last.

He'd lost her. He'd lost her.

God. No.

One more manic puff…and her lashes fluttered.

Relief scudded through him. He picked up her head and cradled her close. "Oh baby. Baby…"

"P-Parker. P-please?"

"What baby? What do you want?"

"Save her." With a trembling hand, Kaitlin pointed to the ceiling, just as a loud thump and a shrill scream rocketed through the house.

Save her?

Fuck it.

He would save them both.

Grabbing a pillow from the sofa, he gently settled Kaitlin's head before racing up the stairs.

He knew what drove him. Knew it. Felt it. Tasted it.

Not revenge.

Vengeance.

And not just for what Tucker had done to Kaitlin.

Vengeance for *all* victims.

He bowled up the stairs, taking them two at a time. It wasn't difficult to find Tucker. He followed the screams. They haunted him. He burst into Kaitlin's bedroom, a place that, until now, had held only the most beautiful memories.

Susan was lying in a disjointed heap by the window, her face bloodied, her body broken. As he watched, Tucker whipped a squirming little girl up into his arms. She must have been three. The tiny cast on her arm scored him.

"No, Daddy, no!" she cried.

No, Daddy, no.

A shiver ran through him. His muscles locked. A little boy's voice echoed in his brain. *No, Daddy, no.*

But he didn't listen. He advanced into the bathroom, holding the gun high, pointed at his wife, Parker's mother. She dropped the towel she was using to dry her son and stepped between her child and this threat.

"Austin. For God's sake—"

A shot. Loud. Sharp. Hideous.

And she fell.

Parker stared at her body. Watched the blood pool from beneath her. His gaze wrenched to his father. A manic fervor lit his eyes. He turned the gun toward Parker.

"No, Daddy, no!"

But he didn't listen.

Another shot. A blazing pain. And Parker crumpled.

The next memory he had was of the smell of gasoline. The cold splashes on his chest and arms. And then flames. Scoring, scorching flames, consuming him. Agony.

It was all he could do to crawl back to the tub, trying desperately to pull his mother behind him. But she was too heavy for a little boy. Too much. And the flames were so hot.

The need to stop the torturous heat overcame him and he released her, released her to the conflagration, and threw himself back into the cooling waters just before he passed out. The darkness was a mercy.

"No, Daddy, no."

That was what would happen to this precious little girl. That was what men like this did.

Resolve settled in his chest. Parker pushed up his sleeves, made fists of his hands. "Put her down." Clear. Cold. Indomitable. A tone he'd never heard in his own voice.

Tucker gaped at him, the rage in his eyes flickering for a moment, and then it flamed to the fore once more. "Rieth? What the hell are you doing here?"

"You're not taking her."

"The fuck I'm not. Get out of my way."

No. Fucking. Way. Parker set himself in the doorway, blocking his path. "You're not taking her. You're not hurting her."

Tucker was bigger than Parker, a great bull of a man. He tried to shove past, but Parker pushed back. "Put her down."

"Fine." Tucker tossed the girl onto the bed. She let out a wail, but Parker ignored her and focused on his opponent. He'd had hundreds in his life—all in the courtroom.

But this was going to be the fight of his life.

He did not expect the blow to his belly. Or maybe he did. He just didn't expect it to be so hard, to stagger him as it did. Tucker landed another punch, and then another, but Parker got in a good one, right in Tucker's midsection.

The bear just laughed and swung at Parker again.

He ducked and the meaty fist swished over his head. But a second followed and hit Parker in the chest, right where it hurt the most. Right where his father had put a bullet into him.

Strangely enough, the pain did not defeat him. It gave him strength, power, determination.

He hauled back and landed a fist right on Tucker's smirking face. Right on his nose.

Blood splattered everywhere. The little girl screamed.

Tucker fell. He fell like a tree with a loud thud.

Parker stood over him, rage boiling in his gut.

Rage, and bone-deep vindication.

In the miasma of emotion, he heard the sirens and he knew, he knew it was over.

He crossed to the little girl who cowered behind the bed. "Are you okay, honey?" he asked.

She threw herself into his arms and wrapped herself around him like a limpet. He carried her over to Susan and bent to check for a pulse. She stirred. Thank God. Thank God, she stirred. Her eyes fluttered open.

"Can you walk?"

She moved. Winced. Then struggled to her feet.

They stepped over Tucker's prone form and made their way downstairs.

Kaitlin, still pale and shaking, met them in the foyer, even as police flooded into the house.

"He's upstairs," Parker barked. The officers nodded and two of them bounded up the stairs. He shifted the little girl on his hip and looped his free arm around Kaitlin and hugged her close, willing his pulse to still. "It's okay, baby," he breathed into her hair. He ran his hand up and down her spine, soothing her. Soothing himself. He'd almost lost her. He'd almost lost her. But he hadn't. "It's all over now. You're safe."

Though his knees shook and his body ached, a great tranquility descended over him. He had Kaitlin in his arms and finally, *finally*, he had exorcized a ghost that had haunted him for years.

CHAPTER SEVENTEEN

Dodging a herd of rambunctious children, Kaitlin carried the last platter of cake pops to the buffet table and settled it in place. She swiped back an escaped curl and looked out over the lawn at the party Emily had created. It was a charity event—Emily loved them—but this one was special. It was for Fostering the Future, the organization that had embraced Parker as a child and made a huge difference in his life.

When Emily had asked her to help, there was no way Kaitlin would say no. The event, a luau, held on the beach of their island home, was a huge success. Tiki torches burned along the surf line and the smell of barbecue rode on the breeze. The evening was cool and clear. Stars sparkled in the sky and the sounds of music and laughter tangled with the low thrum of conversations.

Drew was there, over on the far side of the beach teaching the boys how to build a fire—raising future arsonists, perhaps. In the past month he'd come to accept the truth about Kaitlin and Parker, though he still needled Parker occasionally. But they'd become friends…after a fashion. Drew had even taken them to meet his father so Parker could personally thank the man who had saved his life.

It had been an emotional meeting, but cathartic for Parker. The last stones in the wall he'd built had come tumbling down. He was now, truly, a free man.

Jamie was there too, over with the girls, playing one last desperate game of balloon volleyball before it became too dark. Lane and Cam were giving rides on the boat.

Other children, all kids like Parker, who were growing up in foster care, sat around in small groups eating and chatting with potential mentors. It was Emily's goal to find each child a special someone who could help them navigate the crazy world they lived in, the way Adam Bristol had helped Parker.

She glanced at Parker, sitting against a tree near the beach, talking to a young boy. His expression was somber. He pulled down the neck of his tee shirt and showed the boy his scars. The boy nodded.

Kaitlin smiled at the sight. Parker, with a little boy. She set her hand on her belly and turned to go back to the house to start cleaning up. The fireworks would begin soon and when those were over, all the children would be heading back to the house and, after all the cooking and preparation, the kitchen was a disaster.

"Kaitlin." Emily sidled up next to her and gave her a hug. "What do you think?"

"I think it was a huge success, Em. I am so happy for you."

Emily beamed. "It did go well, didn't it?"

"I know Parker appreciates it. So much."

"I was happy to do it." She selected a pickle and popped it into her mouth. "How are you two doing?"

She tried for a casual response, but failed. The elation welling up within her would not allow it. "Wonderful."

"I am so happy for you."

"I'm happy for you." Emily and Ash's relationship was moving along as well. And now that she knew him better, Kaitlin adored him as much as she loved her friend.

"Has Parker found a job yet?"

"Not yet." Kaitlin glanced back over at him as he stood and solemnly shook the boy's hand. "He's had some offers but...they just didn't feel right." She shrugged. "I don't care. I love having him at home."

Emily stilled. "At...home?"

"Oh, didn't I mention? He moved in with me."

"He...moved in?"

"It didn't make sense for him to keep the lease on his apartment. And we were spending every night together anyway." Every night. All night. It had been glorious.

"I, ah, see. Well, I hope he finds something soon."

Kaitlin shot her friend a knowing smile. "He will."

"Of course he will." Emily said. Then she made a face and put her palm on her belly.

"Are you okay?"

"My…stomach's been upset lately."

"Really?" All right, perhaps the sarcasm was not necessary. But Emily knew her better than that.

Indeed, she flushed. "Okay. I might be a little…pregnant."

"Only a little?"

Emily laughed. "Only a little. But enough to make me queasy. Are you shocked? Because my mother will be. When she finds out."

Kaitlin shook her head. "Of course I'm not shocked."

"Oh good."

"I've known since the day you came home from the island with him—"

"What?"

"Your energy was different. All…swirly."

"I remember you said that. I didn't understand what you meant. Why didn't you clue me in?"

She smiled. "It's your journey, Ems. And may I repeat? I am so happy for you."

"Thank you." Emily wrapped her in a fierce hug. Kaitlin was delighted that it wasn't uncomfortable in the slightest. It rarely was anymore when she touched someone. Another gift Parker had given her.

"Oh, there's Ash. I better go grab him. And Kaitlin, thanks again. For everything."

"Anytime." She watched her friend skip across the lawn, her aura swirling like mad, causing Kaitlin to wonder if she might be having twins.

She bit back a grin. Kaitlin had been seeing a swirly aura in the mirror every morning herself. The inexpressible elation danced back through her and her grin blossomed.

A warmth came up behind her, encircled her. Hard, strong arms wrapped around her waist. "Mmm, woman." Parker's low voice sent a shiver through her. "I've missed you."

"I've missed you too." Because of the influx of visitors, all the boys had stayed at Ash's house and the girls over at Lane's. In the interest of propriety, with all the children around, they'd thought it best to spend the nights apart. "But we've got tomorrow."

"We've got lots of tomorrows."

"Lots. Lots and lots." She turned in his embrace and kissed him. "How are you enjoying the party?"

He leaned his forehead against hers. "It's been incredible. These kids are...amazing." He chuckled self-consciously. "I want to adopt them all."

"Hmm." She looped her arms around his neck and stroked his nape. "We'll have to get a bigger house."

He stilled, stared down at her. "Do you...want children?"

"Not all of them." She giggled. "But I think we would be good foster parents. We'd be good parents."

"We would be."

"How do you feel about that?" She was certain she knew, certain he'd changed his mind about never being a father, but she needed to ask. "Do you want children?"

His expression went somber. "I do. Very much."

Her heart lifted. Her soul sang. "That's good to know, because—"

"Parker!"

Kaitlin turned as an older man climbed toward them on the rise. With delight she realized it was Adam Bristol, looking handsome and hale and, *good gravy*, tall. Much taller than he had been in the hospital bed.

Parker rushed forward to wrap him in a bear hug.

Adam laughed. "Well, what did I do to deserve that?" he asked.

"I'm just so glad to see you're better, sir."

Adam punched him on the shoulder, but not very hard. "Don't sir me, Parker. It makes me feel like an old man."

"Yes, sir— Um. Adam."

"How are you doing, my boy?"

"Very well. You remember Kaitlin? She came to visit you in the hospital?"

"Of course. The pretty thing." He engulfed her in a hug and Kaitlin was nearly swamped by the wave of his vigor. But there was no pain. And yes, he was feeling better.

"I'm so glad to see you on your feet," she said looking up. Way up. "My, you're tall."

His chuckle rolled around them. "Yes, I prefer being on my own two feet as well. Wonderful event, eh, Parker?"

"Yes…Adam. Wonderful."

"Emily did a fine job."

"She did."

"I should hire her. I would hire her, if she'd take the job. She won't of course." Emily's father was a bazillionaire. Besides, she loved doing charity events. "Speaking of hiring excellent people…I understand you're no longer with Barstow and Rank." Adam gored Parker with a sharp glance. It tore Kaitlin up to see him shrink a little, into himself, as though he'd disappointed someone he admired greatly.

"Yes, sir. I was fired."

Fired. Heavens, she hated that word. Something rather militant rose within her, the urge to defend him, perhaps. She slipped her arm around Parker's waist and said, "He was let go for saving a woman's life."

"Yes." Adam stroked his lip. "I heard all about it. All I have to say is, good on you, Parker."

"Sir?" His head snapped up.

Adam set his hand on Parker's shoulder. "I can't tell you how proud I am of you for sticking to your guns and doing what was right, rather than what was right for your career. Not easy to do sometimes, I know."

"I, ah… Thank you, sir."

"But that leaves you out of work."

Parker shoved his fists into his pockets and rocked up on his heels. "Yup."

"Well…" A glint sparkled in Adam's eyes. "It just so happens, we have a vacancy in our legal department."

Kaitlin gaped at him. The lie was so obvious, she didn't understand how no one else saw it. There was no vacancy in the legal department of the Bristol Coffee Company…none but the one Adam had just created.

"A…vacancy?" Parker's throat worked. "But my specialty is divorce law…"

Adam shrugged. "It would be different, but I think you'd be able to adjust. Think about it."

"I don't know... I..."

"Just think about it. We would be honored to have a man like you on our team."

With that, Adam Bristol sketched a wave, then turned and made his way back down to the beach where Ash and Emily chatted with his wife and younger son.

"Wow." Parker scrubbed his face, but he couldn't scrub away the smile. "That was unexpected."

"Mmm."

He glanced at her. "It was unexpected, right?"

"Well..."

His chortle danced on the breeze. "You knew."

"I *suspected.*"

He wrapped her in his arms again and tugged her close. "Minx."

"I told you everything would be all right."

"That you did."

"But Parker..." She fiddled with his collar, unable to meet his eye. "There's something I need to tell you."

"What is it?" His voice was warm, soft. Adoring.

She knew so much, but how to tell him this was a mystery. "Those children we were talking about earlier?"

He looked over at the beach where all the foster children were waving sparklers at the cloaking night. "Yeah?"

She tipped his chin back. "Not those children. The other children. *Our* children..."

His smile froze. His eyes darkened. A little muscle clenched in his cheek. He leaned back and peered at her belly and arched a brow.

She nodded. A tiny bob.

His Adam's apple made the long journey down and back up his throat. He said nothing.

"Are you...angry?"

"A-angry?"

"There's... I can't read..." she waved a hand at the tumult his aura had become. Slowly it settled into a soft, blazing blue.

"I'm not angry, baby." He pulled her back, cradled his hips against hers. "I've just never been so..."

"So, what?"

"Happy. Just, happy."

Fireworks exploded in the sky as he dropped a kiss on her lips. "I love you, you know."

"I know," she said with a wink. "I do. I'm psychic, remember?"

ABOUT THE AUTHOR

Her Royal Hotness, Sabrina York, is the New York Times and USA Today Bestselling author of hot, humorous stories for smart and sexy readers. Her titles range from sweet & sexy to scorching romance. Visit her webpage at www.sabrinayork.com to check out her books, excerpts and contests.

BOOKS BY SABRINA YORK

Tryst Island Series—Steamy Contemporary Romance
Rebound, Book 1
Dragonfly Kisses, Book 2
Smoking Holt, Book 3
Heart of Ash, Book 4
Devlin's Dare, Book 5
Parker's Passion, Book 6

Anthologies and Collections
Five Alarm Fire (High Octane Heroes)
A Cowboy for Delilah (Cowboy Heat)
Saving Charlotte (Smokin' Hot Firemen)
Stone Hard Seal (Hot Alpha Seals: Military Romance Megaset)
Whipped (Brought to his Knees Collection)

Short Stories/Novellas
Extreme Couponing, Fierce, Pushing Her Buttons, Man Hungry,
Rising Green (Horror), Training Tess, Trickery

Wired Series—Steamy Contemporary Romance
Adam's Obsession, Book 1
Tristan's Temptation, Book 2
Making Over Maris, Book 3

Noble Passions Series—Steamy Regency
Folly, Book 1
Dark Fancy, Book 2
Dark Duke, Book 3
Brigand, Book 4
Defiant, Book 5

Fantasy (Romance)
Lust Eternal

www.ingramcontent.com/pod-product-compliance
Lightning Source LLC
Chambersburg PA
CBHW060823120626
46557CB00001B/343